"How long, Laurel—how long since you've been kissed?" Thane demanded.

Her heart turned over. Something uncoiled inside her, spreading warmth throughout her body, her being, her soul.

He deftly removed the pins from her bun. Laurel's dark cloud of hair swirled over her shoulders, tumbling down to her waist.

"Lord, you're gorgeous!" Thane's hoarse voice was full of awe as he spoke and moved close to her, his hand tilting her chin up. Blue eyes nailed her and demanded a response. He leaned down, his lips drawing ever closer. His gaze burned into her, making her skin come alive. Sparks cascaded over her as the wizard worked his magic.

"Wrap your arms around me, Laurel," he said as his lips brushed her ear. "Let me love you."

"Thane, I won't let you do this to me. Don't take away my peace..."

"Laurel, honey, your eyes look at me like that and I know what you want. Your lips part for me. You're like a package all wrapped up and tied and put on the closet shelf. I'm going to untie the strings, and open the package, peel away the layers you've wrapped around yourself—because there's a passionate, loving woman inside..."

WHAT ARE *LOVESWEPT* ROMANCES?

They are stories of true romance and touching emotion. We believe those two very important ingredients are constants in our highly sensual and very believable stories in the *LOVESWEPT* line. Our goal is to give you, the reader, stories of consistently high quality that may sometimes make you laugh, sometimes make you cry, but are always fresh and creative and contain many delightful surprises within their pages.

Most romance fans read an enormous number of books. Those they truly love, they keep. Others may be traded with friends and soon forgotten. We hope that each *LOVESWEPT* romance will be a treasure—a "keeper." We will always try to publish

LOVE STORIES YOU'LL NEVER FORGET
BY AUTHORS YOU'LL ALWAYS REMEMBER

The Editors

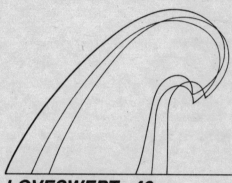

LOVESWEPT · 48

Sara Orwig
Beware The Wizard

 BANTAM BOOKS · TORONTO · NEW YORK · LONDON · SYDNEY

BEWARE THE WIZARD
A Bantam Book / June 1984

LOVESWEPT and the wave device are trademarks of
Bantam Books, Inc.

ISBN 0-553-21658-9

Published simultaneously in the United States and Canada

PRINTED IN THE UNITED STATES OF AMERICA

O   0 9 8 7 6 5 4 3 2 1

To an editor who took a chance, who gave me a chance, who threw away the guidelines and opened wide the doors . . . to C. N. with many thanks.

One

In Shreveport, Louisiana, the sun was shining on a beautiful fall day as Laurel Brett Fortier emerged from her blue Honda. She didn't see the storm clouds gathering on the horizon or hear a magic tune wafting with the breeze. For the fourth time she checked the address noted on a small pad to reconfirm that she was at the right house. There wasn't a mistake. Raising her head, she let her gaze sweep past the inviting yard with its spreading oaks and tall pines to the house. Burned, it was a blackened char. Soot-covered brick walls stood beneath a few black timbers and a fluttering canopy of plastic which served as a makeshift roof. Windows were boarded up, the porch a charcoal gray disaster. Yet on the drive sat a shiny bright red MG, silent testimony that someone was home inside the ruin.

She thought about the conversation with Thane Prescott; it was the first time in her experience as a patent attorney that she'd had someone inquire about toys and games. When he had given her his address, she had thought it was this house, which

1

had burned a few days ago and was just three doors down on the next block from her own home. Then she decided she must be thinking of the wrong house—Why would he want to meet her in a pile of ashes?—and had said she would stop by to talk to him. Now, seeing that she had been right in the first place, she wished she had told him to bring the information to her office.

Clutching her brown alligator briefcase with the initials L. B. F. in gold on the clasp, she started up the walk. Each second her trepidation increased. She wrinkled her nose as the acrid smell of ashes assailed her. How could the man stay in such a place? Suddenly she wanted to get the information and get away quickly. She reached the bottom step of the porch and gazed at it in dismay. The blackened wood, cracked and sooty, looked as if it would crumble if she placed her toe on it.

Dismay teetered into anger. She wasn't sure she wanted Thane Prescott as a client—a man who invented toys and lived in a burned house! She glanced around the yard at the trees. A tire swing was tied to one limb of a pine. Two bluejays flitted past while a redbird's clear whistle could be heard.

She reluctantly crossed the charred porch to reach the doorbell. Smoothing black hair fastened securely in a chignon, she looked down at her immaculate, tailored, beige cotton dress, neatly belted around her waist, and her beige high-heeled pumps. She could imagine what the soot would do to them. Feeling like an idiot, she called, "Mr. Prescott! Yoo, hoo, Mr. Prescott!"

A jay's shrill cry answered. She started to call again when the door swung open and she faced an enormous shaggy gorilla.

Her heart jumped. Gasping, she stepped back as

she gazed into a hairy black face with blue, blue eyes.

"Hi." The voice came from the gorilla, a deep, masculine baritone. Mr. Prescott, no doubt. What kind of lunatic was he?

Taking another step back, gathering her jangled nerves, she answered coldly, promising herself never, never again to go to a client's house. "Mr. Prescott?"

The blue eyes changed. Other than the woolly gorilla hair, she could see only those eyes, but she knew his expression had changed. The twinkle left and was replaced by something else. Curiosity, perhaps? His lids lowered as his gaze traveled to her toes, then returned to her face.

For an instant she became totally aware that there was a man inside the gorilla suit. The thorough appraisal was blatantly male and caused a feminine reaction that made her want to smooth her hair into place. Disturbed, she asked, "Are you Mr. Prescott?"

Black fur shook as his head nodded. "Please come around to the back."

She wanted to get in her car and go. She didn't care to sit down and discuss business with a man dressed in a gorilla suit. "It shouldn't take long, Mr. Prescott, if you'll just step out here."

He laughed. "I don't bite. Come around to the backyard." The door closed.

As she stared a moment at the burned door, her aggravation increased. But she had come this far, she might as well talk to him. She turned to go to the back. Stepping over rubble, burned shingles, broken glass from the windows, she rounded the corner. How could the man live in such a mess? How could he afford her fee? An idea struck her and she stopped, then walked ahead grimly. If he was perched in a tree, she wasn't staying to talk.

At the back corner she paused cautiously. Arms akimbo, Mr. Prescott, in all his woolly glory, stood beside a tall oak. For a moment her attention was distracted. Feeling as though she had stepped through the looking-glass, she glanced around the yard. A large tent was erected beside a pine. A miniature train, like the one at the local amusement park that was large enough to carry people, sat on a track and she recalled hearing its whistle when she was home, wondering which neighbor was causing the racket. Four lawn chairs waited in the shade, one chair already taken by a life-size stuffed rabbit. Toys, boxes, smoke-damaged furniture littered the yard. She had an absurd urge to run.

"Come join me." Thane Prescott rubbed his head, making the black fur swirl in disarray. She approached him warily. He was enormous. Surely the suit had padding. His fur-covered shoulders were wide enough to turn a Cowboy lineman green with envy. He towered over her, at least six to eight inches over six feet, far taller than her five-seven height. But his blue eyes took all her attention. Deep, clear blue, they were magnetic, compelling.

He extended a black paw. "Miss? Mrs. Fortier?"

"Mrs. How do you do." What do you say to a gorilla?"

"Please have a seat." He scooped nuts and bolts off a yellow lawn chair to give her a place to sit. Behind her there was a sharp-voiced, "Hello, hello. Wow, toots! What legs!"

Brett spun around to see a cage hanging in the branches, a bright red, yellow, and green parrot swinging on a perch. "Excuse Manuel," Thane Prescott said. "He says that to everyone—women, men, and children. He must've belonged to a lech-

erous sailor, but I'm trying to teach him an accept-
able vocabulary. Here . . ."

She straightened, wishing she could think of an
excuse to get out of Mr. Prescott's yard, away from
him. He held the chair and reluctantly, she sat
down beneath an oversize toy bat that hung from a
tree limb. Placing her briefcase in her lap, she
gazed up at him. He stood in front of her, arms
folded over his broad furry chest. She suspected
she heard laughter in his voice when he said, "I'm
really harmless."

His blue eyes weren't. "I'm here on business Mr.
Prescott. If you'll give me the information, we'll be
through in seconds."

"Can't wait to go, can you?"

His question added to her irritation. "As a matter of fact, you're a little unorthodox."

"Not your typical client? I would've guessed most
inventors are quite unorthodox." His blue eyes
assessed her thoroughly again and her hand
slipped over her knees, smoothing her skirt until
she realized what she was doing. As if they had
been burned, she yanked her fingers away and
heard a chuckle. "But then," he continued, "you're
not what I envisioned as a patent attorney. Not at
all."

The last was said in husky tones that unnerved
her. He turned to a small table, on which sat a
pitcher of lemonade and three empty glasses. He
poured her a drink, ice clinking as it tumbled into
the glass. He handed it to her, then poured
another.

"No," he said, concentrating on his task," I
expected someone dull, bookish, and male. Not
gorgeous gray eyes, long legs, and definitely"—he
paused to assess her again—"oh, so definitely
female."

She drew a sharp breath, wondering about the man beneath the gorilla suit. It was ridiculous to be so jarred by only eyes and a voice. She took a sip of the delicious cool drink, then heard a rustle. She looked up into the oak branches behind Thane Prescott to find two big blue eyes peering at her.

Startled by the disconcerting stare, she tipped her glass. A trickle of icy lemonade poured onto her shin, running down her leg. "Oh!"

"Here, sorry." Thane Prescott snatched up a napkin and handed to her.

Embarrassed, Brett mopped her leg, glancing up to find him studying her legs. "Need any help?" he asked.

Effortlessly, he had shattered her composure. The laughter in his voice increased her aggravation as she rubbed furiously. "Someone's in your tree. . . ."

He looked up. "Ronnie?"

With another rustle of leaves a small face appeared. "Dad . . ."

Startled, Brett looked up. The man had a family. A family had to live in this rubble. Her heart went out to them as she watched Thane Prescott reach up and swing a small boy down from the tree. Below a mass of red curls, wide blue eyes, and a thin, pale face, the boy wore a red cape, a blue shirt, and bright blue tights. At the sight of Brett, he looked down at his worn sneakers.

A black paw dropped to his shoulder. "Mrs. Fortier, this is Ronnie Prescott. Ronnie, meet Mrs. Fortier." Brett forgot the spilled lemonade. Thane Prescott's voice changed, holding a note of such warmth that she looked at him in surprise.

Ronnie said, " 'Lo." His greeting was a whisper while his solemn blue eyes glanced up for an instant. Before they lowered, Brett felt a shock.

Ronnie Prescott's wide eyes were filled with too much timidity. She gazed intently at the slender child standing in front of her. In spite of all the toys in the yard, he looked miserable, shy in the extreme. And his father's voice held unmistakable concern. "Want some lemonade, Ronnie?"

"Yes, sir."

Brett felt something twist inside. The old hurt resurfaced, catching her off guard. The child seemed so vulnerable, too subdued. But then a man who dressed as a gorilla might be an intimidating father.

"Let's see those hands," Thane said. Small hands raised, black and covered with soot. "How about washing first?"

"Yes, sir," Ronnie mumbled, and he disappeared into the burned house. Brett wondered what kind of woman was inside. How could she live in such a house? Or with an idiot who dressed in a gorilla suit? Was she in costume too? The thought was disturbing. If one more gorilla appeared, she was leaving.

She turned back to Thane. "Your wife's in there?"

Blue eyes leveled on her again and his voice sounded rough. "She's dead."

"Oh, I'm sorry." It was even worse than she'd imagined: That poor little boy had to live alone with this crazy man.

"It was a car accident. It's been almost a year now," he said brusquely. He touched her briefcase with his hairy paw. "L. B. Fortier. What does L. B. stand for?"

"Laurel Brett."

"Laurel. What a lovely name." His husky voice sent a ridiculous shiver along her spine. Whatever his appearance, his voice was incredibly sexy.

"Thank you." Thoughts of the child living in such a place were tormenting her and she forgot the purpose of her visit. "How can you live in that house?"

"We don't. We live in the tent," he said whimsically.

"Good grief." She looked at the large green canvas tent beside a pine. "You don't have insurance?"

She heard laughter in his voice. "Yep, I do, but all the motels in town are full—Shriners' national convention this week—so Ronnie and I stay in the tent and use the bathroom facilities in the house. There's the stove." He waved his hand toward a grill.

Her heart turned over for the child. To live in a tent, alone with this nutty man, eat off a charcoal grill and have to bathe in a burned house . . .

She glanced beyond his fence, down the block, and saw the tops of the pines in her yard. Ronnie's big blue eyes and pale, drawn face haunted her. They needed a place to stay at night. During the day Thane Prescott would be at work and Ronnie would be in school. Her big, roomy house was so close. "If it's only until the Shriners leave, why don't you stay at our house? We live behind you on the next street, Fairfield, only three houses down from here."

Her gaze returned to his woolly face and she immediately wanted to take back her invitation. What on earth had possessed her to ask this . . . gorilla to move in? She knew what it was, the child.

Thane's blue eyes gleamed with curiosity. "That's mighty generous. Won't your husband be surprised?"

"I've been a widow for years."

Something flickered in the blue, changing. "For years?" A hairy paw reached out to tilt her chin upward. "You must've been a child bride."

In spite of shaggy black brows and the ape face, his blue eyes held their own current of magic. She felt as if she had been plugged into a sizzling circuit. "No, not really." She took another breath to make her voice sound normal. "I was in law school; I was twenty-four years old."

"That couldn't have been years ago."

His voice was unbelievably sexy. "It was five years ago," she said a bit shakily.

"Well, well."

He had the wrong impression, so she added hastily, "I live with my younger brother and my father, Judge Webbly.

This gorilla a guest of her staid, rigid, conventional father? When would she learn to keep a lid on sympathy? Maybe if she didn't mention it again, Thane Prescott would forget her offer. "Now, what is it you want to patent, Mr. Prescott?"

Once more, she detected amusement in his voice. "A game and a robot. Tell you what, let me get you some more lemonade and while you drink it, I'll change."

Curiosity overcame her. "Mr. Prescott . . . do you usually dress that way?"

He looked down and rubbed his chest. "You don't like my appearance?"

She clamped her lips together. She should have known better than to ask.

He laughed. "Simmer down. Your big gray eyes give you away. I've been going through boxes of things we pulled out when the house caught fire. I found this and put it on to amuse Ronnie."

As he refilled her glass she glanced at her watch, wrinkling her brow. While he changed, she would be wasting time, and then would have to rush for the family dinner in celebration of her father's birthday.

"Mr. Prescott, I don't mind if you don't change. Just give me the information and I'll be on my way." As fast as possible. There was something going on that made her want to leave. Besides his weird appearance, every clash with his blue eyes jolted her.

"Fine," he said cheerfully. "Actually, the zipper's stuck on this suit or I would've been out of it in time for our appointment. Just a minute."

She watched while he crossed the yard in a jaunty, long-legged stride that didn't bear the remotest resemblance to any ape in a zoo. She wondered what the rest of him looked like—red, curly hair like his son? She couldn't conjure up any image. He disappeared inside the tent and she glanced at the house, wondering where Ronnie was, why he hadn't returned for his lemonade.

She wanted to leave. Thane Prescott made her nervous. The whole yard made her nervous. She expected something to spring at her any minute. She eyed the black bat overhead, then looked at the tent.

Carrying a handful of papers and a box under his arm, Thane Prescott emerged from the tent. As he approached, she prayed he would forget or turn down her offer. She couldn't take him home. Judge Jackson Pierce Webbly would have a stroke! If he didn't, then Harriet Bradshaw, their maid, would. Brett knew even her seventeen-year-old brother, Horace, wouldn't care for a gorilla. But Horace was somewhat of an egghead, a computer whiz who barely knew there was a world outside of his room. A breeze ruffled tufts of black fur on top of Thane's head. Oh lord, why had she asked him to come stay at her house!

"Hi, Toots!"

She looked up at the beady-eyed parrot, the perfect pet for this screwball family. "Get lost, Manuel," she couldn't resist answering.

Thane Prescott heard her and laughed. "Has Manuel been flinging obscenities at you? He's a foul-mouthed bird, but we're working on him." Pulling a yellow chair close to hers, Thane smoothed the papers on his lap.

Hoping it would discourage him, she tried to keep her tone businesslike, cold. "As I explained on the telephone, I need details about your inventions, drawings of them. I'll have to search to see if your toys are duplicates of items already patented."

He sat with one furry knee touching hers, his blue eyes steadily watching her. "Fine," he answered. "I've looked into it, of course, and I don't think there's anything on the market today like my toys."

"There's not anyone like you either." Why had she said that? The man had the most disarming effect.

He laughed. "Or you, Mrs. Fortier." His voice lowered. "You have the biggest gray eyes I've ever seen."

A flurry of sparks went off inside her. "Thank you." In spite of feeling ridiculously pleased, she continued briskly, "As I told you over the telephone, this is expensive." She wondered if he would pay his bill. How would anyone know what to expect from a man who dressed as a gorilla?

"I think it'll be a good investment," he answered with cheery confidence.

"You understand it's money lost if I find your toys duplicate ones already on the market?"

"Sure. It's amazing, you live right behind me and we've never met. I've heard of your father."

"Well, I'm down the block several houses."

"So you're widowed, live with your father and brother. What do you do for fun?" His blue eyes zeroed in with a directness that unsettled her.

It was definitely time to leave. She slipped the papers into her briefcase, hoping to get away quickly, praying he would refuse her invitation. "You ask rather personal questions."

"I'm just that kind of a gorilla."

Startled, she glanced at him, then returned to pushing papers into the briefcase.

"You know, Mrs. Fortier, you're solemn as hell."

Aggravated, she paused again. "This is a business call."

"You need to relax. How about staying? I'll throw some hamburgers on the grill. I'll even get out of this gorilla suit."

What an incentive! She shot him a look before she snapped her briefcase shut. "Thank you, but I have a dinner engagement." If only he would decline moving to her house . . .

He rose when she did. She faced an enormous, black, shaggy chest. He was overpowering, particularly his steadfast blue eyes. Beneath their watchful gaze something fluttered inside. "I'll start the search on these items," she said. "If I need further information from you, I'll call."

His voice was soft, amused. "Wouldn't you like to see the actual items?"

Shocked that in her hurry to get out she had overlooked something so necessary, she felt an unaccustomed warmth flood her cheeks.

"Of course. My mind was on the time."

"He must be important."

Flustered momentarily, she answered, "He's my father. It's his birthday."

"There isn't another important man?"

"Where are the toys, Mr. Prescott?" she asked sharply.

He picked up a small box with multicolored buttons. After flipping a switch, he pressed a button. Whirring noises commenced, then a clanking. She turned to look for the source of the commotion and for a moment forgot Mr. Prescott. Entranced, she stared at the small, furry robot ambling toward her.

It was covered in brown fur, had short legs, short arms with tiny hands, a bright red nose, pointed brown ears, antennae, and large, green glass eyes. While Thane Prescott moved a switch, it ambled to Brett, then halted in front of her and extended a hand.

The voice was high-pitched, squeaky, slightly fuzzy. "Hello. I'm Bzzip. I want to be your friend."

She turned to Mr. Prescott. "How adorable!"

One blue eye winked at her. "Shake his hand."

She picked up the hand, feeling something wiry beneath the soft brown fur. Again the squeaky voice said, "Nice to meet you. I like you."

"My word!" She studied Thane Prescott with new respect. Beneath the monkey suit there was a brain. Not a run-of-the-mill brain, she conceded, but a brain nonetheless. "Won't that be too costly to market?"

Woolly hair jiggled as he shook his head. "It's expensive, all right, but not beyond the level of a certain market. It can stay within the top price range of toys."

"It's marvelous!"

The robot's hand extended toward her again. "Will you come play with me?"

She couldn't resist. She patted his head. "Sorry, some other time."

"Too bad. I want you for a friend—"

"How did you do that?" She interrupted the robot and Thane pressed a switch. "How did it know I said I wouldn't play?"

Thane chuckled. "He held out his hand and you didn't take it. If you had taken his hand, you would've had a different response." He pressed a button and the squeaky voice came to life.

"What do you like most of all in the whole world?"

"Hmmm, most of all? Children."

"That's great. I want to see your room."

Suddenly she realized she'd conversed with a toy. The nuttiness was contagious. She definitely needed to get home. Turning to Thane Prescott, she said, "That's remarkable. What about the game?" His intent blue stare took her breath away. He lowered his dark lashes, but not before she had caught his curious gaze. She wondered how much she had revealed in her answer to the little robot. Thane Prescott pressed a switch and put the box away.

"I'll get the game."

He produced a box and opened it, then stood beside her to show her the contents. She gazed down at a large square of leather, colored with diamond-shaped patterns, and four marble cubes about an inch in length.

"It's called Victory, but it's based on an ancient game played by the Greeks. The details and rules are in the papers I gave you." His voice changed, lowering as he exhaled. "Ahh. You're wearing either *L'Air du Temps* or *Chanel*."

She tried to ignore the fluttering response she

felt as she laughed. "Evidently you don't spend all your time in a gorilla suit!"

He chuckled. "Which perfume?"

"*Chanel.*" A little red flag of warning popped into her mind. This strange man could guess her brand of perfume! And his blue eyes just as easily detected too much about her thoughts. Struggling to keep her voice impersonal, she stepped away from him. "Now, I have your drawings, the specifications, and descriptions, so that's all I need right now to start my search."

"My, you're eager to finish this business."

Eager was an understatement. He bothered her terribly. She felt as if she were dealing with an unknown quantity in Mr. T. Prescott. She picked up her briefcase, telling herself she had to be polite. She had made the offer to stay at her house; now she must ask if he would accept. Please, God, let this man say no, she prayed silently as she looked at his shaggy face.

There was an awkward pause while they stared at each other. She couldn't escape and she thought she saw a twinkle in his eyes. Taking a deep breath, she asked, "Do you want to stay at our house?"

"Well, that's generous of you."

She felt like groaning. Why? Why had she asked him! Whatever had possessed her, child or not? She looked around. "Where's your son?"

"He's shy." The clipped answer didn't hide the concern he'd shown earlier with Ronnie. Then his voice changed, growing lighter as he took her hand in a big paw. "Mrs. Fortier, Laurel? Do you go by Laurel?"

"No, I don't." She looked down at the strands of black fur on her skin. His hand dwarfed hers.

"You don't like the name Laurel?" There went

his sexy, husky voice again, and her pulse went with it, racing away in the most absurd manner.

"My father started calling me Brett. I think he wanted all boys."

"I'll call you Laurel," Thane Prescott said softly. "It's beautiful."

"Thank you." She felt a rush of pleasure. She looked into those deep blue eyes and couldn't breathe. A faint, magical tune wafted in the air. Bells tinkled. Bells? She blinked. "I hear music."

"And so do I," he said huskily.

Her breathing didn't improve. Bemused, she said, "I feel like I'm in the Enchanted Forest." She definitely heard bells. Her wits caught up with her and anger surfaced. "Where are those damned bells?"

His blue eyes mocked her. "It's a toy of Ronnie's."

She felt vast relief, but it faded fast when he added, "Laurel, thank you for the invitation to stay at your house. We accept."

Two

Her heart sank. The day became a low point in her life. She pulled her hand out of his, got caught in pools of blue, and asked the second most ridiculous question of the day. "Would you like to come for dinner?" She held her breath.

"You said it's your father's birthday dinner—we'll come later. We won't bother anyone."

Thank God for small favors. The words, "We won't bother anyone," echoed in her mind. Said so cheerfully. So convincingly. She was to remember those words the rest of her life. She said, "We're the second house from the corner—the one with the portico over the drive."

"Oh, sure. We'll be over around eight. Thanks a million. A real bed will be heaven."

In the distance thunder rumbled. For a moment they both looked at the graying sky, then Thane Prescott said, "Your invitation didn't come a moment too soon. I'd just as leave not stay out in the rain."

He fell into step beside her as she started for the

front. When they reached a pile of blackened rubble he scooped her into his arms without warning.

"Mr. Prescott!"

"You'll get your shoes covered with ashes." He carried her easily, but she felt ridiculous. With a shock, she realized he must be a very large man. There wasn't any padding beneath the suit. She could feel his heartbeat, his warmth, his hard, solid body.

She moved an arm cautiously around his neck. "I feel like Fay Wray. Won't your neighbors raise their eyebrows?"

He chuckled. "Mrs. Danby is ninety-five and couldn't hear twenty tons of TNT blow up. On the other side, the Eastmans are broadminded."

Her family wasn't. He set her on her feet beside her car, placing his paw on her shoulder. "Bye, Laurel. See you later."

"Goodbye, Mr. P—"

"Thane."

It was final, no arguments allowed. "Thane. See you later."

She climbed into her car, glancing in her rearview mirror as she drove away. She saw him walking around the house. Dazed, she felt as if all colors had just deepened slightly. As if the sun now rose and set at a slightly different angle. The meeting with T. Prescott had been a close encounter of the *what kind*? What kind of man was under that silly suit? In a few hours he'd be under her roof. "Oh lord," she groaned. In all the conversation, she hadn't asked what he did for a living, where he worked, what kind of background had. The fumes from the house must have done something to her brain. Fumes or blue eyes.

Turning the corner, she gazed at the wide, tree-filled lawn that sloped to the street from the huge two-story Georgian house that was her home. The neat landscaping, the house itself, exuded money, privacy. She always felt relieved when she got home, as if she had reached a haven of safety, but tonight the feeling was replaced by dread. How would she ever explain Thane Prescott to her father? It was so unlike her to ask a stranger to stay. What had happened to her? She knew. It was Ronnie who had triggered the emotions she thought were finally gone. She shook her head. Regretfully, she saw her brothers' cars on the drive. Everyone had arrived, both older brothers and their wives, the whole staid, rigid, conservative lot of them.

Thunder rumbled again, clouds gathering overhead to darken the sky. Brett's spirits darkened as swiftly.

Minutes later, as she looked over her family, her reluctance deepened. Her father, just an inch under six feet, gray-haired and balding, stood talking to his sons, Jordan and Lamont. Their wives, Nadine and Doris, both blond and wearing designer dresses, sat on the beige silk sofa. Engrossed in a multicolored Rubik's cube, Horace sat in a chair near them. His head was bent over the cube, straight locks of black hair hid his eyes. When she stopped in the doorway, everyone looked up except Horace.

Her older brothers were carbon copies of her father. Prematurely gray, they wore glasses and were pale from constant work in the law office. Their flawlessly tailored suits were silent testimony to their success. They would be just as pleased with Thane as they'd be if she brought home a hobo who had hopped the last freight.

Steeling herself, she greeted everyone, then said, "If you'll excuse me, I'll freshen up."

Doris shook her golden hair away from her heavily made-up face and smiled. "You couldn't look fresher, Brett."

"Brett's a perfectionist," Nadine added. "As a matter of fact, perfect isn't quite good enough."

Accustomed to Nadine's sharp tongue which leveled barbs at everyone except Judge Webbly, Brett ignored her. She had her own problems anyway, at least a big, shaggy one. "Dad, I've offered our house to a client for a few nights."

Every eye in the room focused on her. Even Horace forgot his cube. She continued hastily, "Mr. Thane Prescott and his son, Ronnie. Their home burned and they can't get a motel room." All she could picture in her mind was a tall, woolly gorilla.

"You asked a man and his son to move in with us?" Her father's gray eyebrows arched over his rimless glasses.

"Good heavens, Brett!" Nadine exclaimed. "What will you drag in next? You've brought in every stray cat in the neighborhood."

"Only two, Nadine, and Harriet gave them a home."

"Who is he? How well do you know him?" her father asked.

"He's a client."

"That means a hell of a lot," Jordan remarked. "He may steal the silver. I wouldn't want to live with some of my clients."

"I'll change and we can talk about it over dinner." She left them, escaping the questions. She had climbed two steps up the broad, curving staircase when she heard a voice.

"Brett . . ."

She turned, Horace stood in the hallway. "A little kid's coming to stay?"

"Yes."

Horace's dark brows drew together. "He'd better stay outta my room."

She wanted to shake Horace. "He will. He's scared of his shadow."

"Oh? What's wrong with him?"

She realized there was one thing Horace might relate to. "His mother died last year."

Her brother's forehead puckered. "Gee . . ." As he disappeared into the living room, Brett hoped she had made an impression. When their mother died Horace had been only seven years old. Pausing on the steps, she glanced around. The men in the family were like the house, cold, austere. She looked at the gleaming oak floors, the dark mahogany furniture. There were few pictures on the walls, no knick-knacks. In contrast, she remembered the yard cluttered with toys, the black bat, a tent, a train.

Reluctantly, she climbed the stairs as remorse billowed and enfolded her like a heavy cape. All the time during her quick bath, while she dressed in a sleeveless black cotton dress and high-heeled black pumps, as she combed her waist-length black hair, then put it up into a bun on top of her head, her dread increased. Every minute brought her closer to the time of Thane Prescott's arrival.

Thunder boomed with greater regularity as the storm approached. Listening to it, Brett felt it was appropriate for the evening's events. She joined the others for dinner, moving from the living room across the hall to the large dining room. Harriet served a green salad and Brett braced herself for the questions as her father settled his angry gray eyes on her.

"Brett, tell me again about our houseguest."

"He's a client."

"What's he look like?" Nadine asked.

Brett's heart jumped to her throat. Seconds ticked past while she sipped her water and replaced the glass. Then, with a determined thrust of her chin, she looked her sister-in-law in the eye and said, "Like a gorilla, Nadine."

"Oh, a man with bushy black hair. Is he handsome?"

"He's just what I said—like a gorilla."

"Big and dark-haired. Sounds interesting."

While Jordan frowned at his wife, Brett wondered if dinner would ever end. The doorbell chimed. As if the wiring were connected directly to her spinal column, Brett suffered an unpleasant jolt. She listened to the melodic bells, each one clanging a stroke of doom. He's here, was all she could think. Thane Prescott was at the door.

For an instant she wondered again what he looked like—tall and thin with red hair? His shoulders had felt incredibly broad when he'd carried her.

Through the wide archway leading to the hall, she watched Harriet pass, walking briskly to answer the summons. Icy numb, Brett sat in silence with the rest of the family as the front door squeaked open. A scream sounded, quickly followed by a male voice. More voices added to the commotion.

"My lord, what's going on?" Judge Webbly said.

"Good God, maybe it's a hold-up!" Jordan gasped, his face growing pale.

Brett's heart dropped. "It's not robbers, Jordan." She knew what it was, who it was—and his arrival was going to be worse than she'd imagined.

"I'll see what's happening," she said. Before she could move, Harriet appeared in the doorway. Beneath gray curls her face was pale, her brown eyes were round circles behind her glasses. Two bright spots of red darkened her cheeks.

"Miss Brett, there's some"—she paused and looked over her shoulder nervously—"some people to see you."

"Thank you, Harriet. If you'll excuse me . . ." Her heels clicked on the floor as she walked around the table. "Go on with dinner."

"I wouldn't miss this for the world," Nadine remarked. The family sat in curious expectation, all heads turned toward the hall. Brett stepped around the corner into the hall to greet the disaster that had entered her life.

Thane Prescott stood just inside the door, still clad in the gorilla suit. One hand held Ronnie's, the other held a suitcase.

Wearing a neat white shirt, blue jeans, and sneakers, Ronnie held a large sack of toys and a birdcage with Manuel in it. Beside Thane was the robot, Bzzip, another small suitcase, and a plastic bag.

Brett closed her eyes. For once in her life, she wished she were the fainting type. Then anger filled her. She crossed to Thane and whispered furiously, "Did all your clothes burn in the fire?"

"I'm sorry. I told you, the zipper's stuck."

"Oh my lord!"

"I could've taken a knife and cut the suit off, but I hated to ruin it. This suit's expensive. . . ."

"God forbid you'd ruin it!"

"I'm sorry. You're angry."

"All my family is here. They're so damned conservative and to introduce you . . ."

"We can wait in the car or on the porch until midnight if you'd rather sneak us in."

He was laughing! She wanted to tell him to go away, to forget her offer, to get back into his cage.

She looked down at Ronnie. A peal of thunder rattled the panes and the child flinched. The first big drops of rain pelted the house. Ronnie turned to look up at her, his blue eyes round with fright.

Her heart melted. "You can stay, but everyone's in the dining room . . ."

"Ronnie's hands are too small to unfasten this zipper. I thought you could—"

"I can't undress you!"

He laughed. "All you have to do is start the zipper. Get it unstuck."

Her mind raced. How could she slip him past the dining room. She might as well try to sneak in a parade, calliope and all. If it weren't for his son, she'd throw him out on his woolly ear!

"Hey, toots!" the parrot called raucously. "Wow! What legs! Gimme a kiss."

"Do something about him!" she whispered, her temper rising.

"Ronnie, drop Manuel's cover over his cage. Look, we can wait outside."

"Not in this rain." She didn't see any escape. She would never, never hear the end of this night! This would teach her to let sympathy overcome judgment! Grimly, she said, "Come along. I'll introduce you and show you to your room."

"You could make the introduction after I get out of this suit."

She weighed the possibilities. Anything would be better than taking a gorilla with a parrot into the dining room. "All right, we'll go upstairs as fast as possible. Let me carry something."

"Courage, Camille," he said softly.

"Now listen, Mr. Prescott, you're pushing your luck!"

Thane handed her the robot. "Here, Bzzip's not heavy."

Brett felt as if she were about to run a gauntlet. Raising her chin, she led the way, marching straight for the stairs, acutely aware of the entourage at her heels. And then, faintly, she heard Thane's baritone voice humming: " 'Onward Christian soldiers, marching as to war . . .' "

"Will you stop!" she hissed over her shoulder, trying to avoid his devilish blue eyes. As they reached the dining room door, she paused, looking into expectant faces. All eyes went past her. Judge Webbly dropped his fork with a clatter, an action that was so unlike him, Brett knew the extent of his shock. "My God! Brett . . ."

With all the dignity she could muster, she said, "I'll show Mr. Prescott and his son their rooms, then I'll introduce him after he's changed. Please, go on without me."

Chin raised, her face on fire, she turned and marched up the stairs with Thane and Ronnie following. She was aware of Thane's keen eyes directly behind her, disturbing her and making her conscious of the black cotton shifting and pulling across her hips as she climbed the steps. Raising her chin, she gritted her teeth. At the top of the steps she glanced down to see Horace's head thrust around the dining room door. He disappeared instantly.

"Bravo!" came softly from behind her.

"No thanks to you!" she snapped as she started down the hall.

Thane caught up with her, chuckling quietly. "You carried that off with great aplomb! Couldn't have done better myself."

"Of all the conceited . . ." She looked up to catch gleeful mischief sparkling his eyes. "I hope this isn't an indication of things to come!" She was beginning to wish all she had to worry about was whether he'd steal the silver.

"Want to show us where to stay?" he asked innocently.

Fuming over the gorilla suit, his teasing, his devil-may-care attitude, she led the way down the hall to a small bedroom. Switching on the lights, she glanced around at the polished floors, the single bed with its brown spread, a small bare dresser, and a rocker. Suddenly she wished it were more inviting for Ronnie.

"This is your room, Ronnie. Your father's next door and there's a connecting bath."

They moved to the next bedroom. Like the rest of the house, the room for Thane Prescott held a spartan air. Furniture was minimal. A four-poster bed was covered with a gray spread. She looked at the bed, envisioning a gorilla lounging on it, crushing the soft material into a thousand wrinkles. She turned to face Thane's deep blue eyes. "This is your room, Mr. Prescott."

"Thanks, call me Thane. Look, it's your father's birthday. We'll tackle the zipper after dinner."

"Oh, no! I won't go down and leave you dressed that way."

He chuckled as he turned around and pointed a hairy finger at the back of his head.

She stared at him in consternation. "You'll have to sit down. I can't see it." He sat on a small mahogany chair, twisting so she could reach his back. Ronnie came to stand nearby and watch. Thane reached to the back of his head, parting the long black fur.

"The zipper's caught full of black fur."

"I had a hard time getting it fastened."

She began to pull, tugging at the fur, working grimly. She wondered again about the man inside the suit. He'd caused more upheaval in the past half hour than her family had experienced in the last five years. A scary little whisper told her she was unzipping a Pandora's box of trouble.

"I'm sorry if I embarrassed you in front of your family," Thane said.

She wondered if he really meant that. He hadn't acted embarrassed, or even subdued. She gritted her teeth, easing black strands free of the zipper. "That's all right, I guess. They don't have one shred of humor, not all of them put together, except maybe Horace. . . . Be still. I always have hope for Horace."

He twisted to look up at her. "Hope for your brother? Are the others lost?"

She blushed, startled at what she had revealed. It was the first time in her life she had voiced aloud her attitude about her older brothers. "No," she finally said, "but life is all a dollar-sign to them." He had the bluest eyes she had ever seen. "What do you do for a living?"

"Nothing," he answered with the same casual cheer as if he'd claimed ownership of the First National Bank.

"You don't work?" Shock rippled in her as she saw the dancing laughter in his eyes.

"Is that a catastrophe?"

"Oh my, yes! Don't expect my brothers to talk to you. How do you—" She realized what she was about to ask and bit back her question. There was something far too disarming about Thane Prescott.

He laughed and turned his back to her. "How do I live? I have some savings."

She closed her eyes. Why, oh why had she taken pity on the man! Unemployed, living in a tent, inventing toys, he was the epitome of all her family disliked. Another horrible thought struck her and she looked at his suitcase and plastic suit bag. "Do you have anything to wear? Do you need . . ." She floundered as he turned toward her again. A devilish gleam tormented her.

Her cheeks burned. "Do you have some clothes left from the fire?" she asked bluntly, worried about what might appear when he came downstairs to meet her family.

"I have a few things."

She wouldn't put anything past him. "Would you like to borrow some of my father's clothes?" she offered grimly. Her father would faint if Thane appeared in his clothes, but the alternative might be just as bad.

"Thanks, I'll manage," he said breezily.

Glancing at the suitcase and bag nearby, she was tempted to ask what he'd brought to wear. She bit back the question, and went back to trying to free the zipper, opening it a few inches. A mass of thick, dark brown curls were revealed. She tugged the zipper a few more inches to the nape of his neck.

He shook his head. "Ahh, that's a relief. Wait a minute." He lifted the gorilla head off and twisted in the chair to look up at her. "Hi, Laurel Fortier."

Something happened to her heart. She stood only inches away from him, his knees touching hers, while she looked down into the thickly fringed blue eyes beneath a thatch of tousled brown curls. His strong jaw and well-shaped mouth with a full, slightly thrusting lower lip, added to his handsomeness, to his fantastic good looks. His dark skin was tanned and his chin was covered with tiny dark bristles. While she studied him breathlessly, stunned by the transformation, white teeth flashed and a dimple appeared in his right cheek.

"Gee whiz," she said in awe.

"What?"

"You're better looking without the gorilla suit."

He laughed. "At least one of the Webblys has a sense of humor."

Dazzled, she smiled. "Let's get the zipper."

"Now that it's started, maybe Ronnie can finish it. I really didn't intend to interfere with your father's birthday dinner."

"It's too late now. Besides, we gave him his presents this morning. Below your neck the zipper is thoroughly entangled. Turn around." She wasn't sure she'd worked up her courage to go downstairs yet. She glanced at Ronnie who stood a few feet away. His eyes wide, he looked around the room.

"Ronnie, don't you want to sit down?"

He nodded and perched on the edge of the windowseat to gaze out the rain-streaked window. Brett felt a tug at her heart. Something about the child seemed so vulnerable, so desperately in need of love, in spite of the fact that Thane obviously loved him.

Her attention returned to the father. She pulled at the zipper, working away black fur. It slid a few more inches, revealing bare, copper-colored flesh. It dawned on her that Thane Prescott might not be wearing anything beneath the gorilla suit, and she gazed in consternation at his smooth, bronzed skin.

"Stuck again?"

His deep, amused voice startled her. She yanked some more, pulling away fur. Suddenly she had a premonition of disaster. She had invited disaster into her quiet home. A cyclone was building. She'd better put up all the barricades, lock the gates, and get set to weather a storm, because one was brewing right under her hands. One with smooth copper skin and brown curly hair. Take cover, an inner voice warned while another tiny voice told her it was already too late.

A knock sounded and Horace stood in the open doorway. Gazing round-eyed at Thane, he said, "Dinner's over."

"Come in, Horace. Thane, this is my brother Horace Webbly. Horace, this is Mr. Prescott and his son, Ronnie."

"Hi." Horace entered the room still staring at Thane. "You been to a costume party?"

"No, I haven't. Ronnie, introduce Horace to Bzzip. He might enjoy that."

Ronnie picked up the box of buttons, flipped the switch and pressed a button. Bzzip clanked to life, marching ahead. Ronnie worked the controls, turning the robot to face Horace. Brett paused a moment, catching Horace as he reached out to take Bzzip's outstretched hand. Horace's voice was awe-struck. "This is yours?"

"It's Mr. Prescott's invention," Brett said.

"Neat!"

"My dad's invented a game, too," Ronnie said.

"No kidding?"

"Yeah, come on, I'll show you."

"Can we take Bzzip?"

"Sure." Ronnie climbed down, pressing a button. "Want to work him?" The two boys headed toward the hall with Bzzip clanking in front of them.

"Well, you made a hit with one Webbly," Brett said.

"That isn't the important one."

He said it so quietly, while she concentrated on the ensnarled zipper, that it took a second to register. Then lightning streaked through her. She tried to sound firm. "Look, I asked you to stay here because I felt sorry for Ronnie."

He turned again, leveling on her those blue eyes that tripped her pulse. "There really isn't a man in your life?"

"No, there's not. I'm about to send you back to your tent, rain or no."

"Why?"

"I think you've misinterpreted my motives."

"I'll try my question again. What do you do for fun?"

"I manage. Turn around."

She worked in grim silence, tugging furiously, anxious to be finished and out of his room. She yanked and managed to catch more strands.

"Nervous?"

Something snapped inside and without stopping to think, she retorted, "Yes!"

He turned back to her. "Why?"

"You're a walking arsenal of exploding amunition! Have you ever done anything quietly in your life?"

The dimple appeared and his gaze drifted to the bed. "Some things," he said, his voice dropping to a suggestive sensuousness.

"Turn around." Her cheeks became hot as his gaze drifted back to her.

"Why the blush?"

"You know—"

He laughed. "Calm down, I'll turn my back so you can get me undressed."

"Mr. Prescott, dammit!"

"Honey, I don't want you to call me 'Mr. Prescott.' "

She worked determinedly, wanting to get away from the man. The zipper finally slipped free, moving down easily and revealing more coppery skin over a muscled back.

"Wow, that feels better."

He wriggled out of the suit, letting it fall around his waist while he turned around. His shoulders were real. They were powerful, bulging with muscles beneath tanned, smooth flesh that was slightly damp with perspiration. Dark brown hair curled in a thick mat on his broad chest, tapering down in a narrow line to disappear beneath the gorilla suit. He was overwhelmingly masculine.

"You can manage the rest yourself," she said hastily.

He rose, clutching the gorilla suit to his flat stomach. A strip of white flesh showed below the tan at his waist. He towered over her, his masculinity, his virile body, his clear blue eyes invading her senses. She became aware of herself, of her crisp black cotton dress, her hands at her sides. Her skin tingled from head to foot.

It took an effort to ask, "Why don't you join us downstairs? I'll introduce you to my family."

"Fine." His eyes continued to hold her; she felt as if she were rooted to the floor. The walls closed in, then faded. Blue engulfed her, slicing through layers of consciousness, through her defenses to touch her innermost being, setting off bells, starting a fire deep within her.

When she drew a sharp breath, his eyes narrowed slightly. Whatever wild magic that had sparked to life in her had touched him too.

He tilted her chin upward. For a moment she had the absurd notion that he intended to kiss her. With a shock she realized she wanted him to. Her gaze drifted to his lips, the slightly full lower lip that looked sensuous, so enticing. And she knew

Thane Prescott's kiss would be devastating—the last thing on earth she needed.

The moment stretched while she studied him. Her lips ached, tingled. He whispered, "Such big, beautiful gray eyes . . ."

"Thank you." Her voice sounded distant in her ears; she didn't have the foggiest notion what she'd answered. His eyes were weaving a spell. Blue wizardry. Beware the wizard, she thought. Reluctantly, she stepped away. "There are clean towels in the bathroom."

"Fine. I'll shower and be right down."

Dazed, she left, feeling a mixture of emotions, unable to shake the image of Thane Prescott's fit male body, unable to forget that wild, surging current sent by his blue eyes. She didn't want to think about the attraction that had flared so fiercely between them. If only her breathing would return to normal, her heart would slow!

Halfway down the steps, she met Greg Hamilton, Horace's best friend. He raced past her with a breezy, "Hi, Brett."

She watched him hurry to Horace's room and realized that she didn't have to worry about Horace disliking the Prescotts. No doubt he had already phoned Greg to come look at Bzzip. Her glance shifted to Thane's door. The vision of him under the shower, his coppery shoulders below a spray of water flashed in her thoughts. Too clearly, she could see the rivulets coursing across his broad chest, matting the thick brown curls. "Ohh . . ." she whispered, startling herself that she had spoken aloud. Thane Prescott was dynamite and wherever he went there was an explosion. She couldn't imagine him in an office, working as other men. Whenever he came on the scene the world turned topsy-turvy. If only her heart didn't, that was the danger.

She reached the hall. Squaring her shoulders, she entered the living room or, more aptly, the den of lions. Her father wasn't in sight so Nadine fired the first volley. "Well, Brett, what was that? You've been to the zoo?"

Lamont stood by the window, gazing into the rainy darkness. He turned. "Brett, who have you brought home? Why was the man dressed as an ape?"

"He's Thane Prescott. He lives around the corner."

"Where's he work?" Jordan asked, settling into a wing chair.

She drew a deep breath. "He invents toys."

"What else does he do?" Lamont asked coldly.

"Nothing." The word dropped like a bomb.

"You've brought home a bum who tinkers with toys?" Lamont exclaimed.

Nadine laughed. "You've done it this time! Of all things, to drag in a man who dresses like a gorilla. Next men with little white nets will be hunting for him."

Jordan frowned. "Prescott? Where's his house?"

"Around the corner, on the next block."

"I think I know who he is. He played football. He was ahead of us in school."

"You're right," Lamont said. "Thane Prescott. I recall now. He went north to college. He was a quarterback. I think he set a record that's still unbroken for the number of yards gained by passing."

That figured, Brett thought. "I don't remember him."

"You're too young," Lamont said dryly. "He must be at least seven years older than you."

"His father was a food broker," Jordan continued, "but both the older Prescotts are dead now. I guess he's come back here to live."

Trust her brother to remember the elder Mr. Prescott's occupation. At that moment her father entered the room. His gray eyes flashed with anger; his face was suffused with red. "Brett, Harriet just quit."

"No!" Harriet had worked for her parents for the past thirty-two years, since Jordan was born. What else could possibly go wrong?

"She said that man said the most obscene things to her at the door."

"Obscene?" Something clicked. That damned dirty bird. "Dad, that was a bird. It wasn't Mr. Prescott."

"A bird?"

"My God! Is there a bird in the house?" Doris asked.

"It's Manuel, a parrot, and he's upstairs in a cage. Thane is a gentleman. He wouldn't insult Harriet." Why was she defending him so stoutly?

"How do you know?" Nadine laughed. "How long have you known him?"

"Since this afternoon," she answered defiantly. "He's a charming man." Why did she keep at it? He was pure trouble.

"Brett, I can't lose Harriet—"

"You won't have to, sir." A deep voice came from the doorway. "If you'll let me speak to her, I can clear this up."

Everyone turned. At the sight of Thane the next charge of dynamite exploded, inside Brett. Dressed in a light brown suit, white shirt, and dark tie, his head capped with the mass of brown curls, he was so handsome he took her breath away. He made the other men in the room fade into gray paper cutouts. His bronzed skin, big blue eyes, flawless clothing, massive shoulders, and height overshadowed mere mortals. He was stunning! Without doing anything, simply standing still, he dominated the room. His eyes focused on her with the force of a gale. She felt the contact to the soles of her feet. She licked dry lips and he smiled slowly.

How he had bathed so quickly, she couldn't imagine, but she noticed the few damp curls over his ears. As she crossed to take his arm, emotions—relief, amazement, but above all, attraction—rippled in her. He was thoroughly male and when he looked at her, he made her feel totally feminine, all woman.

Her voice sounded breathless as if she had run around the block instead of merely crossing the living room. "Thane, I'd like you to meet my family."

"Sure." He smiled and said in a low voice, "Thanks for rising to my defense. 'Charming'?"

She blushed and clamped her lips together. Emotions shuffled and anger surfaced. As they crossed the room together she was aware of his clean scent, an enticing aftershave, his muscled arm beneath the soft material of his sleeve. She dropped all concern about his impression on her brothers. Thane's flawless suit and shirt looked more costly than theirs, probably the only fact that would register with Lamont and Jordan.

"This is my sister-in-law, Nadine, another sister-in-law, Doris . . ."

Nadine straightened and Doris smoothed her blond page-boy hairdo. At the look of shock in Nadine's eyes, Brett felt a twinge of grim satisfaction, then moved on.

"Thane, this is my father, Judge Webbly, and my brothers, Jordan and Lamont."

Thane said hello, shook hands with the men,

then said to her father, "Sir, if I may have a word with your Harriet, perhaps I can make amends."

"A parrot, eh? It won't hurt to try."

The two men disappeared down the hall and Brett knew what the outcome would be. How could Harriet resist that smile or dimple? For an instant there was a stunned silence before Nadine looked at Brett. "You've been holding out on us perhaps?"

"I just met him a few hours ago, Nadine."

Conversation picked up again when her father returned. In a few more minutes Thane rejoined them, entering the room with the same dynamic force as before, his presence gathering attention like a magnet picking up metal. He blithely announced that Harriet had agreed to stay. He talked with the men, and while Brett sat facing Doris and Nadine, she caught snatches of conversation. As her father and brothers listened to Thane discuss a new oilfield in south Louisiana, Horace, Greg, and Ronnie appeared in the doorway. One look at the three pale faces and Brett's brief peace of mind smashed to bits.

Three
___

She rose. "Ronnie, come meet my family." After introducing him quickly and introducing Greg to Thane, she glanced at Horace, who continued darting frantic looks over his shoulder. What now? A feeling of dread filled her, along with a reluctance to ask Horace why he looked so worried. Suddenly she wondered if they had broken Bzzip. "Is something wrong, Horace?"

"Yeah." He licked his lips and jammed his hands into his slacks. "The parrot's gone."

Doris sat forward on the sofa. "Gone where?"

"Manuel's loose?" Thane asked quietly.

Ronnie answered. "Yes, sir. He got out."

"You let a bird loose in here?" Smoothing her blue silk dress, Doris rose to her feet. "I loathe birds."

"I opened his cage," Horace said.

"Horace, for God's sake," Judge Webbly snapped.

"I'll look for him," Thane said. "He's too large to lose."

"My purse is in the library. I'll get it and then we're leaving, Lamont. I can't abide feathers."

Doris left the room, turning to the right down the hall. Brett had a sinking sensation. Why couldn't life stay normal around Thane? He hadn't let the parrot out, her brother had, but there wouldn't be a parrot loose in the house if it weren't for Thane Prescott.

As if he could read her thoughts Thane glanced at her, lifted his broad shoulders in a shrug, and winked. He actually winked like a fellow conspirator. He was enjoying the uproar! Damn him, anyway—the uproar was his fault!

"Sorry, but Manuel's harmless," he said to Lamont. Then he crossed the room and dropped his hands on the shoulders of Ronnie and Horace. "C'mon, guys, let's search for Manuel."

"I'll help," Brett said, a conviction growing that she better stay with them, that disaster threatened. They started up the stairs while Lamont, Jordan, Nadine, and Judge Webbly talked in low voices in the hall.

Suddenly, a woman's shrill cry shattered the quiet.

Down the hall Doris emerged from the library. Her cheeks had spots of bright red as she clutched her purse and half-ran toward them.

"Lamont! Oh . . ."

"Doris, what on earth?" Lamont faced her, his brow furrowed angrily.

"I've never, never been told such a foul thing in my life!" Doris saw the group on the stairs and stopped, giving Thane a look that made the boys scamper up a few steps. "You pervert!"

"Doris!" Brett was so startled by her staid sister-in-law's behavior, she scarcely noticed her father disappear into the living room.

Doris shook with rage, raising her purse to wave

it angrily at Thane. "You pervert, teaching a bird such talk!"

"I'm sorry if he offended you," Thane said innocently. Brett shot him a look, but he gazed blandly at Doris.

"Lamont! I hate feathers—and then to be told, to have suggested by that feathery monster . . . oh . . ."

"Let's go." Her brother looked at Brett. "You have strange tastes, sister dear."

Anger mushroomed inside her. "It's only a bird, Lamont."

Nadine stood in the living room doorway, her dark eyes filled with curiosity. "Doris, you can't leave without telling us what he said."

"For heaven's sake, Nadine! It was the most vulgar, unspeakable obscenity."

"That's Manuel, all right." Thane descended the few steps to the hall. Brett heard laughter in his voice and her aggravation increased. "Which room were you in?" he asked Doris.

Brushing past Nadine and Jordan, Judge Webbly reappeared, carrying a large pistol. "Now, where's the damned parrot?"

"Dad . . ." Ronnie came down the steps. "Is he gonna shoot Manuel?"

"No, Ronnie."

"Dad, put away the gun," Brett pleaded. Why had she invited the Prescotts to stay? "Thane will catch Manuel." Hastily, she took Thane's arm. "Come here. Doris was in the library. It's next to the living room."

With the boys, they entered the library and heard a squawk. The parrot was perched on a brown drapery rod near the ceiling. "Awk! Pucker up. Gimme a kiss, babe!"

Thane took off his coat and shoes and stepped

onto the brown leather sofa; his soft tan slacks pulled tautly over hard muscles. Nadine stepped into the doorway. "Jordan and I are leaving now. Good night, Mr. Prescott, Brett, boys."

Her dark eyes rested on Thane until he turned to smile at her. She waved at him, then disappeared into the hall.

Thane looked at his son. "Ronnie, run get the cage."

As all three boys left, Thane said, "Why don't you close the door so he won't get out of this room."

"Awwk! Gimme a kiss! Hey, babe . . ."

With a flash of white teeth Thane looked down at Brett. "Better plug up your ears, sounds as if he's on a talking jag."

"I'm not as delicate as Doris."

He stood with his hands splayed on his hips, his feet spread apart on the sofa. "You're not, eh?"

"No, but dammit, you're about to ruin my home life!"

"You're angry?"

"That's so strange? Why would I be angry? You almost made Harriet quit. She's been with us over thirty years. You insulted my sister-in-law, aggravated my father, disrupted my peace. . . ."

"Want me to pack and go?"

She was tempted to answer yes, yet he looked so damned appealing standing there in his socks, his white shirt tapering to his narrow waist, blue laughter capering in his eyes.

"Send Ronnie out into the rain to sleep in a tent?" he added.

"You have a sneaky streak." An urge to smile fluttered inside her.

"Sneak, sneak!" Manuel screeched. "Awk!" The door opened and the boys appeared. Behind them stood Judge Webbly. He peered through his glasses at Thane.

"Good night, Mr. Prescott, Brett, boys."

"Good night. Happy birthday, Dad."

"Thanks, Brett. Thank you for the bookends. I leave tomorrow for Caddo Lake for my fishing trip, remember?"

"Oh, I'd forgotten." It was a miracle she could remember her own name, she was so addled by Thane.

"I'll see you in the morning," Judge Webbly said. He closed the door while Ronnie handed Thane the cage. Brett watched as Thane climbed onto the arm of the sofa, bracing one stockinged foot on the back. It was impossible to keep her gaze from drifting down the length of him where his slacks were molded to his bent leg, his thigh.

"Come here, Manuel," he called softly.

"There's a cracker in the cage, Dad."

The bird squawked, uttering a foul obscenity that convulsed the boys and turned Brett's cheeks bright red. After quelling the boys with a stern look, she had to bite back a laugh as she watched Thane slowly extend the cage, talking quietly to Manuel. His white shirt was stretched across his broad shoulders and she remembered how they had looked when he'd peeled away the gorilla out-fit.

Suddenly the parrot started to flap away, but Thane's big hand closed around its neck and he shoved it into the cage, slamming the door shut. Manuel batted his wings, sending a flurry of red feathers flying over Thane.

"Bastard! Awk!"

The boys snickered. Feeling a need to set an example, Brett frowned. "Horace!"

With pantherish grace Thane dropped lightly to

the floor. "Here, Ronnie, take the rascal to your room and put the cover on his cage. You better get into bed too."

"Yes, sir. Will you be in?"

Thane reached out to squeeze his son's shoulder. "Sure, after a while."

"Horace, it's about that time," Brett added. Horace and Greg both nodded. As the boys left, she said, "Want another cup of coffee, a drink, some wine?"

"A glass of wine might be nice."

She crossed the room to a small bar. "Red or white?"

"Red, please." He followed her, leaning one hip negligently against the wall, his arms folded over his chest while his gaze drifted over her in a leisurely male appraisal that set nerves quivering. One light burned in the room, giving a soft glow to the brown furniture, the walls of bookcases, an intimacy to the situation. Acutely aware of him, of his steadfast watchfulness, Brett opened a cabinet, pausing when he asked, "You're really angry with me, aren't you?"

Her stormy face focused on him. "You came into this house like a cyclone. The dust hasn't settled yet."

"Why do you live here?"

Starled, she gazed wordlessly at him for a minute. He was staring at her so intently she felt he could discern her soul. "It's home."

"Yeah, for Horace, for you when you were a child. What do you do at night? Sit in here and read?"

"As a matter of fact, I sometimes do." Her annoyance increased and she turned away from him, pulling an unopened bottle of red wine from the cabinet. A trapped feeling began to envelop her and she grabbed a corkscrew and started working on the cork with more determination than finesse.

Finally, as if drawn by a magnetic force, she looked up. His deep blue eyes reset her inner works, speeded her pulse, hampered her breathing.

"Besides reading," he drawled, "what other hobbies do you have?"

"I like to garden." She tried again to screw the corkscrew straight into the cork, frowning as she worked. "I like to dig, to watch things grow. . . ." She glanced up again. His knowing smile made her feel as if she had revealed more than she'd intended. Grimly, she bent over the bottle again.

Tanned fingers reached out to take the bottle from her hands. With competent ease he twisted the corkscrew, pulled, and removed the cork.

"Thank you." Swiftly, she poured the wine into two glasses, handing one to him. His warm fingers locked over hers, his touch starting a current in her fingertips that swept through her.

"You're hiding from the world here," he said softly.

"No!" she flung back angrily. "This is home. It's a nice home, so roomy it would be ridiculous for me to stay elsewhere. Horace needs me."

"Horace will go to college soon, I imagine. I made a quick tour of the upstairs. I saw your room."

"Your wine," she reminded him, hoping to change the subject.

He smiled as if fully aware of his hand on hers. His eyes held magic; his smile bewitched her, the dimple appearing, creases deepening. Then he took his drink and moved away, breaking the disturbing contact. Picking up her own glass, Brett walked toward a chair. Thane sat down on the sofa and reached out swiftly to take her arm. "Sit down here, Laurel."

Even though his touch was light, his voice brooked no argument. She wanted to pull away, to sit in a chair out of his reach. He was so incredibly masculine and his questions were too probing, but refusal was impossible. When she sat down on the opposite end of the sofa, a fleeting smile crossed his features, making her feel ridiculous for scooting as far as possible from him. After folding her long legs beneath her, tucking the black skirt neatly over them, she faced him.

"Wow, what legs," he said softly, mimicking the parrot. "Manuel has good taste."

"I'm beginning to miss the gorilla suit."

He raised his brows. "Why?"

She shrugged. "It was a barrier between us. You have a way of watching me that's . . . intense."

"You're a fascinating subject," he drawled softly and a warmth uncoiled, enveloping her, yet adding to her wariness.

"I can't be. Back off, Thane."

"Oh, but you are. Your soft black hair, your big gray eyes that are far too solemn. You look as solemn as Ronnie."

"Don't look at me as if I'm a new project."

He stretched his long arm across the back of the sofa and touched her shoulder lightly with his fingertips. It was the merest touch, yet his hand became a flaming torch, searing her skin. His husky voice added to the reaction caused by his fingers. "A project? Oh, no. You're thoroughly female, honey. A flesh-and-blood, real live woman in spite of . . ."

She frowned, annoyed, yet too curious to resist asking, "In spite of what?"

"You tell me," he answered softly. "As I said, I saw your room."

Torn by a mixture of emotions, she tried to inch away from his hand. The thought of Thane in her room disturbed her. "And . . ."

"It could be a room in a Holiday Inn. It's about that personal." He leaned forward and cupped her chin in his fingers. "What're you hiding from?"

"Nothing." Her annoyance increased along with a sudden panicky feeling. She didn't want his questions, she didn't want to analyze what she felt, her motives. He was so big, so male, too close physically, moving in too fast on her emotions.

"Your enormous gray eyes give you away. You're hiding from the world in this house. You're in a shell, Laurel Brett Webbly Fortier." The names rolled softly off his tongue, in a languid baritone. "Patent attorney, gardener, widow, daughter, sister . . . woman." He said the word "woman" in husky tones that conveyed a smoldering sensuality. "Will the real Laurel please come forward?"

She jerked her chin from his fingers. "You're just accustomed to the never-never land you live in! Talk about hiding, Thane! You live in a world of toys, you don't earn a living. How long since you had a job?"

"Five months. I quit." He straightened, settling back against the sofa, holding the glass of wine on his knee.

"Do you know how unrealistic that is? What happens when you use up your savings?"

He looked amused, disconcerting her. Suddenly, she realized how little she knew about him. "By that time, my toys will be on the market."

"Well!" She drank her wine swiftly. "As they say, people who live in glass houses . . ."

". . . should use solar energy."

"Can you ever be serious?"

"Occasionally. You're getting in a huff over a few questions."

"I'm not in a huff."

"I didn't see a picture of your late husband in your room. What was his name?"

"Wade. We met, became engaged after two months, married after three months, he developed a blood disease and died by the sixth month." She recited the familiar explanation swiftly, without emotion. "It happened so fast, it seems like a dream now. Something that never really happened." She took a deep breath. "It's getting late. We'd better synchronize our schedules." She knew she was talking too fast. Thane leaned back against the sofa, giving her full attention with eyes that were far too knowing. He was so big, his broad shoulders, his long legs, his large hands disturbed her senses. His unorthodox ways, his sensitivity alarmed her. She didn't want him to examine her life.

"I have to be at work by nine, Horace goes to school at seven-thirty."

"Laurel, how long is your hair?"

Breathless, she paused. "It's to my waist."

"Do you ever wear it down?" he asked huskily.

"Only to bed." The look that flashed into his eyes destroyed all rational thought. For an instant she stared at him blankly, forgetting what she had been saying. A slow smile lifted the corners of his mouth and drove her to recollection. "Now, look," she began, then paused, took a deep breath, and tried again. Her breathless voice steadied only a fraction. "Dad leaves by eight-thirty, except tomorrow he's going on a fishing trip so he'll be home until later in the morning." Thane sipped his wine while his mocking eyes watched her. She continued, "Harriet comes at seven to cook breakfast. Since you don't work—"

Thane choked on his wine, then looked up as he swallowed. "The disapproval in your voice—oh my!" He laughed.

"You have a son you're responsible for. Anyway, what time does Ronnie have to be at school?"

Thane shrugged his broad shoulders. For an instant she could picture him playing football; he had the rugged build for it, the muscles, the brawn, the long legs. He settled back into the cushions, stretching those legs in front of him, angling them toward her. It was an effort to keep her gaze from drifting down the entire length of him. "It doesn't matter about us," he said. "Ronnie doesn't go to school. I teach him at home."

"You *what*!"

"I teach him." He sipped the last of the wine.

"Why doesn't he go to school?"

His dark lashes lowered swiftly and when they raised, a shuttered look hid any expression in his features. "I can do just as well, if not better, because this way he has a lot of individual attention. I'm home. He's had a traumatic year and he's had to make a lot of adjustments."

"Well, there's more to it than that!"

Thane sat up straight, crossing his legs, one ankle on his knee. He rested one hand on his ankle and she looked at his strong, blunt fingers, the wide gold wedding band. "It's legal," he said brusquely. "My application was approved by the State Department of Education. When he enrolls in the Caddo Parish school, he'll have to take a test, that's all."

"That wasn't what I meant. Even if you're a good teacher, there's the social side. He needs to learn to get along with others."

"He will," Thane answered. The defensiveness in his voice was so plain it twisted her heart. She felt aggravated and sympathetic at the same time. "He has a lifetime to socialize with people," Thane added.

"But this age, this year is so formative, so important. He should be with other children. Look how shy he is."

Thane's jaw hardened, a muscle working in his cheek. She ached for him. With a swift movement he rose to his feet. "As you said, it's late."

"Now who's evasive?"

"Look, I know my son and what he needs."

"Thane, he needs other children."

"He'll be with them, next year when he's had time to get over the shock of losing his mother." His fists rested on his hips, his jaw had a slight thrust as he looked down at her defiantly.

"But can't you see that he might get over her absence sooner if he has other children around? If he gets out of the house more?" The cold, shuttered look told her clearly how little her words meant. "Have you seen anyone professionally, a therapist, a counselor?"

"Yes, immediately after the car wreck, after I lost Pam, I took Ronnie to a counselor," he answered flatly.

"And . . . was it recommended to keep him at home?"

"I've seen two counselors." Each word was clipped. His voice grated as if it were painful for him to talk. She listened, wishing she could do something to help them both, to help Ronnie, to stop the look of angry frustration in Thane's eyes. "We lived in Cleveland until two months ago. Ronnie had counseling there and again when we moved here. The one in Cleveland said to send him to school. The one here said it would be all right to keep him home."

"You're not doing Ronnie any good."

"Look, he needs me. I was an engineer. . . ."

A noise sounded in the hall and they looked around to see Ronnie in the doorway. Dressed in pale green pajamas, he faced Thane. "Dad, I left Freddy and Bubba in the yard. They'll get wet in the rain."

Brett looked at Thane questioningly.

"Freddy and Bubba are stuffed bears," he explained. He turned back to Ronnie. "Are you sure they aren't in the tent?"

Big blue eyes gazed solemnly at Thane as Ronnie shook his head. "No, sir. I left them in a box under the charcoaler. They're gonna get ruined. . . ." His voice quivered.

"Hey, Ronnie, I'll get them. You go back to bed and I'll bring them up when I get back."

"Will you? Oh, boy!" It was the first time Brett had seen Ronnie's smile and it was as engaging as Thane's. Dimples appeared in both cheeks before he turned to disappear down the hall.

"It's pouring."

"Freddy and Bubba are important."

"Want a flashlight or a raincoat?"

Suddenly he smiled and even though it vanquished all the tension, she wondered what he had been about to say when Ronnie appeared. The moment was gone, but she felt as if she had missed something important in getting to know Thane. The dimple appeared, tempting her to smile in return.

"I'll run change into jeans, but I didn't bring a raincoat," he said. "If you have one and a flashlight, they'll be handy."

"I'll see what I can find while you change." In the

hall when they parted, she paused, watching him walk away, his long legs moving in a purposeful stride, his back straight. He looked invincible and strong. Ronnie appeared so frail and vulnerable, yet she wondered if, beneath the surface, Ronnie had a tough streak and Thane was vulnerable. His defensiveness about his son was unmistakable. He turned at the stairs and their gazes locked. With a shock she realized she was staring. She headed for the kitchen, embarrassed that he had caught her studying him so openly.

Minutes later he appeared in the kitchen, dressed in a pale blue knit shirt and jeans. The blue flattered his dark skin, matching his eyes, and again she felt breathless looking at him. Each time he entered a room, he overpowered his surroundings. The off-white kitchen, its off-white formica table and counter and white appliances, paled, were diminished by Thane's vitality. An aura of virile masculinity radiated in waves that washed over her, sweeping her with their force. Her gaze was caught by his and she forgot what she had started to say.

She blinked rapidly, turning away with an effort to break the spellbinding hold. Behind her, he said softly, "Laurel . . ."

Desperately, she looked down at the yellow slicker in her hands. She faced him, holding up the coat like a shield to protect her from a dragon. A very handsome, blue-eyed dragon. "Here's an old raincoat of Dad's and a flashlight."

"Thanks." His warm fingers closed over hers, sending a shower of sparks radiating from the contact. She met his heavy-lidded gaze and experienced another burst of fiery tingles. He tilted her face up and her breathing became constricted. "The bears will be soaked," she whispered.

"What bears?" he asked in a husky tone. "Oh, yeah. Gray eyes dazzled me and I forgot what I was doing. Just completely forgot."

His words worked their own sorcery with her heartbeat. She pulled away from him, stepping back to watch while he pulled on the coat.

The yellow slicker strained across his shoulders and the sleeves reached just below his elbows. He laughed. "Afraid this won't do. Just give me the flashlight."

He dashed into the storm and Brett closed the door. She stood at the window, watching as lightning flashed, illuminating the yard with a silvery brilliance. For an instant she saw him running down the drive, his long legs stretched out as he leaped over a puddle. He seemed to barrel through life, to meet everything head-on. She wasn't sure she could understand the onslaught of his seductive attention.

She made hot chocolate, waiting until he finally returned with a bag under his arm, his dark curls in tight ringlets about his head.

"The bears are safe, but I'm dripping and muddy."

"Here's a towel. Step to your right, into the utility room. I've made hot chocolate and there's a robe in there you can wear, so just put your clothes into the washer."

"Such efficiency! I'm impressed. Would you like to give these to Ronnie?" He handed her the plastic bag and took the towel to rub his curls dry.

Opening the bag, she removed two worn toys—a brown bear with amber glass eyes and a stuffed panda. She held up the bear. "I haven't seen a teddy bear like this in years."

"It was mine."

She laughed, unable to imagine Thane Prescott

as a child, much less as a child with a teddy bear. When she looked up, she was startled to see him pull the wet knit shirt over his head. His wet jeans were molded to his trim hips and hard legs. With the shirt gone, his shoulders glistened damply; the dark mat of hair on his chest tapered to a narrow line beneath his wide leather belt. He was overwhelmingly sexy. Flustered, she raised her eyes and caught him watching her. She turned away abruptly.

How he moved so fast she never knew, but silently, without seeming effort, he was beside her. He put up his arm, blocking her. The kitchen wall, his arm, his body, the refrigerator cornered her.

"Thane . . ."

His voice was a husky rasp, hoarse with sensuality. "You're not going to run from me."

"No . . . don't . . ."

"How long, Laurel?"

"How long, what?"

His free hand reached up to touch the bun on top of her head. "How long since you've been kissed?"

Four

Her heart turned over. Something uncoiled inside her, spreading a warmth throughout her body, her being, her soul. And fear, an inordinate, unreasonable fear that something was about to occur that she couldn't control, blossomed, shaking her, making her tremble.

"Thane . . . don't . . . Get out of my way. Really out of my way."

"You're cheating yourself. I want an answer." He ran his big fingers into the hair on top of her head. With deft, delicate movements, he shifted his hand, wriggling his fingers, and pins tumbled onto the floor. Her dark cloud of hair swirled over her shoulders, tumbling down to her waist.

"God, you're gorgeous!" His hoarse voice was full of awe. "Your hair is beautiful." He caught a strand to run it over his cheek.

"Thane, please," she whispered. She couldn't breathe. The temperature had jumped forty degrees. She felt on fire. His biceps bulged beneath smooth brown flesh, his forearm was covered with a sprinkling of dark hair. His broad, masculine chest was inches away. She could smell the wet clothing, his clean scent. She felt assaulted by maleness, by his probing eyes, his insistent, personal question.

He tilted her chin up. "How long?"

"Since Wade died." The answer was torn from her. She didn't want to think about that time, the emptiness since then. The pain had been so unbearable. She had locked it away forever.

"Oh, Laurel, all those years . . ." His voice held such pain-filled wonder, she forgot her agony to look at him in surprise.

"Not once? How have you kept the men away?"

"It wasn't difficult. Until now," she whispered. "I don't go out often and when I do, it's someone safe. . . ." What was she saying? She could only watch his lips part, see the smoldering longing in his eyes, the penetrating gaze that seemed to read every thought in her mind.

He leaned down, his enticing lips drawing closer. His curly lashes lowered almost over his eyes, stopping short so he could watch her with a heavy-lidded gaze.

Her lips parted a fraction. Beneath such a look she couldn't possibly keep her mouth closed. His gaze burned into her, making her feel everything. Nerve ends sprang into existence, quivered, felt alive, so alive. Sparks cascaded as the wizard worked his magic.

She licked her dry lips. "No, Thane," she pleaded.

"No? Laurel, you're saying 'yes' with every ounce of your being. Open your mouth for me. Give me your kiss, honey."

His lips touched hers.

A touch. Flesh against flesh. It was the key to her emotions, to the vault that had guarded her feelings, her sensuality. She felt floodgates open inside as his lips parted hers, his tongue invaded, captured, claimed her. His wild, yet tender sorcery blanked out everything else. A kiss—a kiss that made the earth quake, that made the heavens rumble.

A moan deep in her throat startled her.

He moved his mouth away, kissing her ear. "Wrap your arms around me. Surely you've had a date in all that time."

She barely heard his question. She was lost in a maelstrom of sensation as his hand moved down her spine, his thumb tracing each vertebra, his fingers sliding over her back.

"Yes," she whispered, moving her mouth to his throat to kiss him. She felt starved, overpowered. She raised her hands slowly to barely touch his shoulders. His skin was smooth, warm. "I've had dates with men who were like my brothers, safe. Nothing sexy, no magic about them. Not like you at all . . . at all . . ." She suddenly twisted her head. "Oh, no! I won't let you do this to me. Don't take away my peace. . . ."

"Laurel, honey, your beautiful big eyes look at me like that and I know what you want. Your lips part for me. . . ." His husky voice wove its own spell. "You're like a package, all wrapped up and tied and put away on the closet shelf. Laurel, I'm going to untie the strings and open the package, peel away the layers you've wrapped around yourself—because I know there's a passionate, loving woman inside."

"Thane, don't . . . just don't," she pleaded softly, yet she didn't want him to stop. Years fell away, haunting memories disappeared. She had guarded against emotions that were surfacing with alarming swiftness. She wanted his arms, his kisses, yet another part of her knew how threatening he was. All her peace, the orderly life she had established was on the brink if she yielded, because deep in her heart she knew with Thane it wouldn't be anything light. He lived life to its fullest and she was certain he would make love the same way, without reservation, without allowing her to hold back anything. She had to do something. Her mind groped for straws; anger was a safer emotion.

She pushed him away, forcing her eyes open to look up at him. "Thane, stop."

Chest heaving, he opened his eyes and her knees almost buckled. She felt overwhelmed by the desire burning plainly in his eyes.

"No!" she gasped and turned away. He caught her in his hard arms, pulling her to him, crushing her, kissing her passionately.

Desire exploded inside her, bursting through her, setting her aflame. She cried in her throat, pushing against the hard chest. Relentlessly he continued, his tongue exploring her mouth, driving away resistance, logic. She felt his heart hammering against hers, she felt the heat from his loins, the dampness of his rain-soaked jeans seeping through her dress.

Finally, she pushed free. In seconds he had stormed the carefully erected barriers, her cool defenses that had withstood everyone for years.

Gasping for breath, she gazed at him and knew that she wanted Thane Prescott more than she had ever wanted anyone. And she reasoned it was simply because she hadn't been loved, hadn't even been kissed in so long. That's all there was to it. Simple physical craving. Get yourself under control, she sternly admonished herself. In a shaky voice she said, "Don't take advantage of me because I offered you a place to stay."

Something flickered in his eyes. He looked hurt as he drew a deep breath, his broad chest expanding. His fingertips touched her cheek lightly.

"Why are you so afraid of life?"

"I'm not. Sex isn't always a necessity."

His mocking blue gaze told her how much he believed her answer.

"Thane, please . . ." She twisted and his arm went out to block her path again. She gazed at the hard, bronzed skin. She raised her finger to trace a scar on the underneath of his arm. "You were hurt."

His voice was hoarse. "I got that when I was a kid. I tried to parachute off the roof."

She looked up at him. "You're not ever afraid of life, are you? Not even the painful things . . ."

He leaned down to pick up the fallen bears. She hadn't realized she'd dropped them. He held them out to her. "Sooner or later I'll get an answer from you."

She shook her head. "You're like the Pied Piper, a spellbinding magician leading me to disaster. Don't—"

"Spellbinding?"

She had admitted too much. And yet she knew it wouldn't be enough for Thane. "I'll take the bears up." She waited, but his arm still blocked her. He shifted his weight, moving closer, but not touching her. She turned her head to one side and drew a deep breath. She felt cornered; her heart pounded.

He turned her face and his sensuous voice held a promise that made her tremble violently.

"Sometime soon I'm going to hold you and kiss you until you tell me what you're afraid of."

"Oh, no!" she whispered. "No, you won't." But she wondered how she could stop him. He was invincible. Did she want to stop him? She wanted him, oh, how badly she wanted his kisses! Yet, all that pain in her past, the promises she had made to herself. Never again did she want to open herself up to the possibility of going through such agony. Never.

He lifted a strand of long, silky black hair, letting it slide through his big fingers. "Someday I'll spread this over a pillow, over my bare shoulders. . . ."

"God, Thane! Stay out of my life!" But, even as she cried out in panic, somewhere deep inside, part of her needed his strength.

In the same tone he continued, "Someday I'll see the laughter in your big gray eyes. All the fear, their solemn look will go. There'll be passion and laughter and—"

"I'll take the bears to Ronnie." Ducking under his arm, she brushed past him and left the room, her heart thudding against her ribs. She clutched the toys to her breast as if they could comfort her.

A boom of thunder shook the panes, making her jump, and she realized how tense she was. Thane's kisses were devastating. Her mouth still held the taste of his, her lips felt swollen, tingling, aching for more.

In dismay she looked down at her dress, damp from being crushed against his jeans. She went to her room, flung off the dress and pulled on a blue cotton robe, fastening its high neck under her chin. Hurrying to Ronnie's room, she tapped lightly, then opened the door.

The room was transformed. It looked lived-in, as if it belonged to someone. A Mickey Mouse night-light gave a soft yellow glow. Manuel's covered cage sat on one end of the dresser. Along with comic books, Ronnie's clothes lay scattered on the floor. The stuffed black bat lay on the dresser beside a small model airplane. Two toy trucks were on the floor. With a rustle of covers, Ronnie sat up in bed, his eyes wide.

"He got 'em." The relief was evident. Another clap of thunder boomed and Ronnie hunched his shoulders, shivering. Handing over the bears, Brett sat down on the edge of the bed. "Which one is Bubba?" she asked softly while she folded the long robe over her knees.

He held up the brown bear, then carefully tucked the panda beneath the covers on his right. Bubba was tucked in the left, then Ronnie scooted down.

Brett straightened the covers. She felt drawn to the little boy, caught as firmly by his big blue eyes as she was by his father's.

"I don't like storms," he whispered.

She shrugged. "It's noisy, but the rain makes plants grow."

"Thunder's scary."

She smoothed the mop of red curls, wondering how this frail child could belong to the powerful man downstairs. "Want to hear a story?"

"Sure."

"I used to tell Horace stories, but it's been a long, long time."

He reached out to touch her hair, running his thin fingers down the smooth strands. "Your hair's pretty."

"Thank you, Ronnie. There's a story about a woman who had long hair only hers was golden."

"Rapunzel." He sounded stricken as he turned his head away to stare at the wall. "Mom used to tell me that one."

He sounded so pitiful, Brett felt a stab of pain. "Oh, Ronnie, I'm sorry."

"I want her back. . . ." He sniffed and Brett forgot herself. She scooped him up and held him close, leaning her cheek against his soft curls. His thin arms wrapped around her and he clung to her while he cried, his sobs a soft whimper in the quiet room.

She felt as if a dagger had been plunged into her heart and someone was slowly twisting it. Tears welled up and she stiffened, fighting them fiercely. She tried to force her thoughts to something impersonal, to business, to anything to keep from remembering. . . . She ran her cheek over her arm to wipe away a fallen tear. A board creaked behind her and she looked over her shoulder.

Thane stood in the doorway, his big fists clenched, his face pale, dark brows drawn together. Her father's robe was belted around his narrow waist, squeezing his shoulders together, the sleeves absurdly short. His chest was barely covered and the robe just reached his knees. He looked ridiculous, but his expression held such hurt that she didn't know who she felt such agony for, father or son. Abruptly, Thane turned and left her with Ronnie.

She rocked the boy, holding him tightly until he stilled. In a soft voice, she began the story of the Three Billy Goats Gruff, finally lowering him to the pillow.

Fringed with wet lashes, Ronnie's wide blue eyes stared up at her, his red curls a tangle over his forehead, while his small fingers played with strands of her hair. She finished the goat story. "Sleepy?"

"A little. Dad says it's okay to cry."

She smoothed curls off his forehead, watching them bounce right back. "Sure it is, Ronnie."

"My dad cries too."

Her heart jumped. Tears stung her eyes and her throat hurt. Fighting the threatening tears, she asked quickly, "Would you like to hear about Peter Rabbit?"

"Yes, ma'am."

While she talked his fingers wound through the ends of her hair. Finally his eyes closed, his hand became still. She tucked the covers around him and rose, tiptoeing out of the room.

In the hall she paused, looking beyond the railing at the light streaming into the hall below. Thane was in the kitchen, no doubt drinking hot chocolate. She didn't want to see him, so she retreated to her room.

She changed into a long white cotton nightgown and climbed into bed staring into the darkness. Mentally, she ticked off the upstairs rooms. The big master bedroom at the east end of the hall where her father slept. Next Horace's small room. A bathroom. Her room, then the small room where Ronnie was and at the west end of the house, Thane's room. She clutched the covers, wadding the sheet in her hands. She lay stiffly in the bed, fighting the pain that threatened to engulf her. Damn the Prescotts. All the agony she had fought, thought she had forgotten, recovered from, hovered on the brink like rising floodwaters. Damned if she would cry! Not ever again. She had shed enough tears to fill a lake. But she hurt so badly. To hold that small, frail body . . . Ronnie was seven years old, only two years older than her child would have been, the baby she had lost in the miscarriage.

Angrily, she flung away the covers. In desperation she turned on all the lights in the room, then picked up her briefcase, sat down at her desk, and went to work. She poured over specifications for a piece of oilfield drilling equipment, something so far removed from Thane Prescott, she hoped to get him and his son out of her mind completely.

It was ten minutes after three when she fell exhausted into bed. At six-thirty she rose, bathed, and dressed in a tailored navy skirt and white blouse, all the time wondering what schedule the Prescotts followed. Fastening her hair in a bun on top of her head, she realized there were probably pins still scattered on the kitchen floor. That would raise Harriet's eyebrows.

She shrugged and headed for the downstairs with a glance at the closed doors of the other bedrooms. It was too easy to imagine Thane stretched on the four-poster, his big shoulders and chest dark against the white sheets. Clamping her jaw closed, she hurried down the steps.

When she entered the kitchen, it was clean with no dropped pins, no cup or pan from the hot chocolate. Thane Prescott had his neat moments.

She started breakfast, heating the oven for canned biscuits, a sin that never failed to bring a frown from Harriet who thought biscuits should be made from scratch or forgotten. The back door opened and Harriet peered into the room.

"Morning, Harriet. Something wrong?"

"Ma'am, is that parrot down here?"

"Oh, no! It's safe. You can come in."

Harriet looked relieved. "Miss Brett, that's a horrible bird."

She cracked two eggs into a skillet. "I know. Mr. Prescott said he's working on cleaning up Manuel's vocabulary."

Dressed in navy slacks and a baseball cap, his

thin chest bare, Horace entered the room. "Hi," he said. "Is my shirt dry?"

"I didn't know you had anything in the dryer," Brett answered as she seasoned the eggs. "Mr. Prescott dried some clothes last night."

Horace disappeared into the utility room. The dryer door banged and she heard a "Wow."

He reappeared holding a bit of black and gold tiger-striped mesh material. "Hey, Brett. Look at Mr. Prescott's neat underwear. What a stud!"

"Oh, for heaven's sake, Horace!"

"I'll bet he taught ol' Manuel to say those things."

"Horace Webbly!" Harriet's face was scarlet.

"Yes, ma'am." Horace disappeared into the utility room and Brett returned her attention to the eggs. But the maddening vision of Thane's bare, virile body dressed in the mesh briefs danced in her mind, sending her pulse racing. Too easily she could see every inch of copper flesh, the dark mat of curls that narrowed over his flat stomach, the pale flesh where his tan ended. . . .

"Miss Brett! The skillet's on fire!"

"Here." Thane was suddenly beside her, turning off the burner. "Where's a lid?"

Feeling like an idiot, Brett opened a cabinet to remove the skillet cover. Thane put it down over the flames.

"There." He looked at her. "Good morning, Laurel."

Out of the corner of her eyes she saw Horace leave hastily with a breezy, "I'm late. I'll skip breakfast." Folding his arms over his chest, Thane continued to watch her. With brown boots, he wore jeans and a white knit shirt. The ends of his curls were damp from a shower; his jaw was clean shaven. He was vibrant with masculine appeal, filling the kitchen with his presence. Beneath his intent gaze, she blushed. She hadn't blushed in years, until she had met Thane Prescott. His eyebrows raised as he watched her cheeks turn pink. "Morning, Harriet." His blue eyes didn't leave Brett's face. "What started the fire?"

She knew Harriet was staring and the heat in her face grew worse. "I guess my mind wandered."

Thane's dimple appeared and she wanted to shake her fist at him, but she curbed the impulse. Harriet took the skillet to clean the burned mess. Brett couldn't free herself from Thane's compelling eyes. "Wandered to where?" he asked, his grin widening.

"You're pushing your luck!" she snapped.

He laughed softly and she knew Harriet had turned to stare again. "Harriet, I'll let you cook the next batch of eggs. I'll make the toast. Will Ronnie be down?"

"Nope. He's asleep. I'll cook his breakfast."

"How many eggs, Mr. Prescott?" Harriet asked.

"Two please. Over easy. I'll get my clothes out of the dryer."

Brett put four pieces of bread into the toaster and pushed the handle down.

While Harriet cracked eggs, she glanced at Brett. "He calls you by your first name. High time someone did."

Surprised, Brett looked at the short, graying maid. "Miss Laurel," Harriet said. "I always thought you should've been called by your first name. Sounds nice."

"Thank you, Harriet." She poured two glasses of orange juice and set them on the table. Harriet had four places set on blue linen mats. Brett sat down and unfolded the morning paper. As she glanced at the headlines, Thane appeared in the doorway of the utility room. "I've lost something," he said, frowning.

"What's that?"

He ran blunt fingers over his mass of brown curls. "My underwear."

Harriet looked stricken. Brett felt another blush starting to rise, along with irritation. "Oh, no."

Thane raised his eyebrows. "You have my underwear?"

"No!" She felt like swearing.

He chuckled. "You know where it is? You have some habit I should know about?"

"Look here . . ." It was becoming more difficult to curb her temper. What happened to a peaceful, uneventful morning? She knew. Thane.

He laughed. "I'm teasing."

Harriet picked up a box and left the room.

"You'll be the end of Harriet." And maybe more than just Harriet.

Thane moved to the stove. "I think the second batch of eggs is about to burn."

"Oh, my goodness!"

"Sit down. I'll watch them. Where's my underwear?"

"I suspect on the way to high school."

Thane's eyebrows arched. "Your brother has my underwear?"

"You made a definite impression."

"Why would he take my underwear to school?"

"No doubt he's wearing it. That's probably why he skipped breakfast. Horace never skips food," she stated dryly.

Thane looked so puzzled she laughed. "I can tell you're not around teenage boys much."

"No, but once upon a time I was one. I can't recall wanting to wear someone else's underwear."

"If you had grown up in a household of plain white shorts, weren't allowed to wear jeans—"

"Horace can't wear jeans?"

She shook her head. "Dad doesn't approve of them. Horace probably wants to show off, impress his friends with those tiger-striped mesh. . ." Her voice faded, Thane's dimple appeared, and she knew she had walked right into trouble."

"Yes? You were saying?"

"To hell with you, Mr. Prescott," she said lightly.

His tone was mocking. "What did you say you were thinking about when you let the eggs burn?"

"Cut that out!"

"That was after Horace found my underwear, wasn't it?"

"Thane, so help me!" She couldn't stop the blush that burned her cheeks. He laughed and turned back to the eggs. Her gaze drifted down his broad back to his tight-fitting jeans and momentarily she vizualized tiger-striped mesh briefs over smooth skin. She shook her head. What was the matter with her?

Harriet returned with spots of pink in her cheeks. She moved around the kitchen, casting oblique glances at Thane. He served the eggs while Harriet put the toast on the table and poured coffee.

Thane sat down across from Brett and smiled. Despite herself, the sun rose in her world and she basked in its light. His dimple, his white teeth, the creases that bracketed his mouth, all added up to an appeal she couldn't resist. She smiled in return. He reached into his pocket and held out his hand.

"Something you left behind."

When she opened her hand, he dropped her hair pins into her palm, and she had a feeling she'd left more than the pins with him. He closed her fingers over them so she wouldn't drop any. His hand on hers, his gaze, the memories he'd conjured up, held her breathless as seconds ticked by. "Did you sleep well?"

Something crashed into the sink and Harriet mumbled, "Sorry."

Brett nodded.

"I saw your light go off around three."

"You were in the hall?"

"I went in to check on Ronnie."

"Oh." She noticed Harriet scurrying into the utility room.

"Did you know the Shriner convention lasts until next Tuesday?"

Startled, she blinked her eyes. "Tuesday? Oh, that's all right." It was Friday. Four more nights with Thane. Her pulse speeded up. His hand still held hers. His thumb drifted across her wrist, paused, then rested on the blue vein beneath her pale skin.

"Your pulse is fast."

She wanted to pull her hand away, but she sat still. "Could be."

His eyes sent messages that speeded her pulse more. His gaze dropped to her lips. She parted them, then whispered, "Thane."

He glanced around the empty kitchen and said softly, "You're all dressed for work, back into your neat, tidy, proper appearance. Your tailored clothes, your hair all pinned up. You look cool, efficient. But underneath I know there's a warm, passionate woman who has long, silky black hair. . . ."

"Thane, don't," she said breathlessly. Her heart was pounding in her ears and she couldn't take her eyes away from his.

"That's one of the things I like about you."

"What?" How could she resist asking?

"Your sexy voice. There are moments when it gets this husky quality. You sound breathless and feminine and warm. Seductive . . ."

Each word wrapped around her like a gossamer thread, weaving a web that bound her. "Please stop," she whispered with all the firmness of cotton.

"I will now because this isn't the place or time, but we'll take up this conversation later."

Even though he released her hand, she was still mesmerized by his words, his hungry blue eyes. He leaned back in his chair, smiling at her, keeping her pulse at a dizzying speed.

The spell ended when her father entered the room. "Morning, Brett, Prescott."

"Morning, Dad." Reality descended, the routine demands returned. She glanced at her watch. "Good heavens, I've got to hurry."

While the two men conversed, she rapidly ate her egg and toast, drank the hot black coffee, and left for work.

Twenty minutes later, when she turned into the parking lot behind the small brick building that housed the firm of Webbly, Incorporated, she didn't feel the usual familiar rush of satisfaction. The office was the brightest spot in her life—a job that was interesting, that kept her occupied, her thoughts busy.

She entered the building and walked down the hall, carpeted in plush bright blue, to greet Marie Anderson, the golden-haired secretray who had been with her family's law firm as long as she had.

Relieved to arrive ahead of Jordan and Lamont, she stepped into her quiet office and gazed at the polished oak desk, the sofa and chairs upholstered in dark blue, without a shred of pleasure. All she could see were big blue eyes with pale lashes, deep blue ones with thick curly brown lashes, father and son. No longer was the office a haven from the world. Not the office or the house on Fairfield. She realized that if she weren't careful, her heart wouldn't be safe either.

After putting away her things, she started the search to see if another robot had been patented, any kind that would make it unfeasible to patent Bzzip. It was difficult to concentrate as she drifted continually into thoughts of the previous night, thinking about the ridiculous bird, about Ronnie's tears, about Thane—his mouth, his kisses, his big, hard body.

Ronnie's eyes haunted her. She knew he belonged in school. Everything about Thane haunted her, his overpowering presence, his laughter, his worried gaze when he talked about his son.

Each time she thought of them, she pulled herself abruptly back to the task at hand until eleven-thirty when her phone rang. When she lifted the receiver she heard Harriet's distraught voice.

"Miss Brett, you father's been arrested."

Five

Brett's eyes widened with shock. "Arrested? Dad?"

"Yes, ma'am. The police were here. Mr. Prescott went out, both of them went out and the first thing I knew—"

"Harriet! Slow down. What's happened? Where's Mr. Prescott?"

"He's gone to the police station. Oh, I can't imagine . . . Judge Webbly. It was that bird, that awful bird. . . ."

"How could Manuel get my father arrested?"

"He was so upset."

"Who was upset?" Another rush of words poured through the receiver and Brett knew she wouldn't get anything sensible out of Harriet. "Look, I'll go to the police station. Stop worrying. Sit down and let your nerves calm."

Brett hung up, then quickly grabbed her navy purse and car keys and left the office.

During the short drive she mentally berated herself for allowing the Prescotts near her family. Her father, a judge, in jail? She could imagine the headlines. Harriet said it was the parrot. That damned parrot. She should have let her father shoot Manuel the night before.

When she reached the station, she parked in the shade of an oak, climbed out, and hurried inside. Within minutes, she discovered that no charges had been filed and that her father had gone home, but nothing more. She headed for the car. The Prescotts would be the end of her. Particularly one Prescott. She was beginning to feel like a long-tailed cat in a room full of rockers. When would the next blow descend? She didn't have long to wait.

Unlocking her car door, she heard a man's voice call "Laurel!"

She straightened. At the end of the block Thane closed the door of his bright red MG and hurried toward her. He was dressed in the tan suit, white shirt, and dark tie. At the sight of him, her heart skipped a beat, starting a fluttering that made breathing difficult. Sunlight caught auburn glints in his dark brown curls. The wind tangled them over his forehead and she could imagine their softness, what it would feel like to touch them.

He covered the distance in long strides, dropping his hands onto her shoulders when he reached her. His voice was wary as he asked, "What did Harriet tell you?"

She ignored the question. "Why was Dad brought down here?" As she spoke she was distressingly aware of Thane's hands on her, his broad, solid chest only inches away.

"I'll tell you about it, but relax. It's all worked out."

She let out a long breath, listening as he continued, "Now look, I'm sorry. You're going to have to teach Horace to keep Manuel's cage door closed. This morning your brother left the birdcage unlatched again."

She closed her eyes a moment. "You know, we used to lead normal lives. What happened?"

"Everything's all right. Let's go to lunch and I'll explain."

"I think I'll get indigestion if I eat now."

"No, you won't. No one's harmed. Not really. We'll go in my car. I have the culprit with me."

Dismay changed to anger. "That damned parrot is in your car? I have to eat lunch with Manuel? No, thanks!"

"I have his cover. We'll tuck him away somewhere." Ignoring her protest, Thane took her arm and headed down the block toward the MG. "This morning Manuel got out. Your neighbor's mother from Scranton is here to visit and she doesn't know your father."

Brett's spirits sunk. She could just imagine what was coming. "When Ronnie woke up, he discovered Manuel was gone, so he went to look for him. Your father offered to help since it was Horace who left the cage open."

"You're sure it was Horace?" Since when did Horace know anything existed except his computer? As quickly as the question came to mind, the answer surfaced—since Thane's arrival.

"He moved Manuel's cage to his room this morning." Thane's long arm stretched out as he opened the door to his car. In the back seat Manuel's beady eyes gazed unwinkingly at her while he sat on his perch in the cage.

She slipped into the car and when Thane settled behind the wheel, she said, "Tell me the rest."

He reached over to touch her cheek lightly. "Don't look as if the world fell apart."

"I'm braced for the worst."

"Laurel, you take life too seriously, you really do."

"Too seriously!" Her frayed nerves snapped. "There's B.T. and A.T.—Before Thane and After Thane! I said last night you came into our house *like* a cyclone—but you *are* a cyclone!" The husky, breathless note in her voice became more pronounced as she revealed her feelings. "When you appear on the scene, you upset everyone, dislodge everything . . . set the world spinning in another direction."

"Do I really?"

"Dammit, don't flash your dimple at me!"

"My dimple bothers you?"

She was shaking, caught in a tempest of stormy emotions. "No! Yes, you're laughing!"

"I didn't even snicker, honey. Hmmm, set the world spinning in another direction." His mocking voice and smothered laughter added fuel to her anger.

"What happened this morning?" she snapped.

"Nothing really disastrous. Your father spotted Manuel in an oak by the house next door. It's nice fall weather, windows are open. Your father climbed the tree to get the parrot—"

"Dad in a tree? I can't picture that."

"Well, he was. I asked him to watch Manuel while I went back for the cage. The tree was outside the window of the room with your neighbor's mother. She heard some of Manuel's choice remarks. . . ." While Thane talked, he pulled off his coat, shaking it out to lay it across the back of the seat. He loosened his tie and tugged it free, then unbuttoned the first two buttons of his shirt. His actions cut into Brett's thoughts about the incident. As she listened, another part of her was noticing how his shirt stretched over his broad shoulders as he moved. She noticed the dark tufts of hair curling on his chest, inviting her fingers to touch. She noticed how his tan slacks molded his long legs. His aftershave was enticing, a fresh scent that was growing familiar. She tried to pay attention to his words, to get her thoughts away from his long, masculine body, but it was impossible. Thane continued and his words flitted through her mind, carrying less meaning by the second until she realized he had stopped talking and was staring at her. Startled, she felt the blush start along her throat, flaming into her cheeks.

"I'm sorry," she began, suddenly aware of the breathless, deep sound of her voice. "What were you saying?"

"What were you thinking?" he demanded, his blue eyes probing.

"I just . . . my mind wandered," she answered, attempting to get her voice back to normal and failing completely.

He leaned toward her. "Your mind wandered? Like it wandered this morning when you burned the eggs? Laurel, I intend to see to it that you stop fighting your feelings. Another string on that package just came undone. I'll get your heart unwrapped yet."

"No, you won't!" She straightened, moving back against the door of the car, crossing her legs and folding her arms over her waist. "Leave me alone, Thane. My heart is in the package and it isn't tied up with strings—it's chained and padlocked and I want it left that way!"

"Sure you do." The drawling sarcasm was gentle. His voice lowered to a seductive huskiness. "Sure thing, Laurel. That's why you're backed into a corner of the car, all but huddled into a ball. That's why you lost your train of thought when you watched me take off my coat and tie. Honey, you're fighting yourself. And I intend to see to it that the woman in you wins the battle."

His words stormed through her system, wreaking havoc. She felt a trembling start inside, radiating through her body, her arms and legs. At the same time a deep inner longing, a hunger so demanding, a need so primitive, responded, sang to life and yearned for Thane to do just what he said. She was torn between desire and dread. Mocking blue eyes watched her inner struggle.

"You're fighting a losing battle. I'll show you." He moved over the shift separating them and wrapped an arm around her slender waist to draw her to his hard chest.

"Thane, not here!"

"To hell with here," he murmured before his lips took hers in a wild, burning kiss that fulfilled his promise. With arms of steel he pulled her into his lap and crushed her to his heart while his mouth drove her beyond protest.

His demanding tongue explored, sending flames dancing in her while reason, embarrassment, awareness that they were parked in front of the police station, wavered dimly in her mind. Her struggles were futile and brief as his arms tightened. His kiss deepened and she no longer cared about anything except Thane.

Breathless, dizzy, she wound her arms around his strong neck, running her fingers sensuously through his thick mat of curls.

He felt so solid, so good. His curls were as soft as she had imagined, tickling her fingers in an entrancing sensation. His heart was thudding against hers and she twisted her hips closer against him.

"Hey!" A male voice sounded behind them.

Thane released her and Brett looked over her

shoulder. A man's head appeared in the window. He raised a camera. "You're Judge Webbly's daughter, aren't you? That's the parrot too!" The head was replaced by a camera, the camera clicked, and the man was stepping away. "Thanks!" he called, then started running down the sidewalk.

Six

With startling swiftness, Thane opened the door and vaulted over her. He was out of the car instantly, running after the man. Seeing Thane after him, the man speeded up. Thane's long legs stretched out and a few seconds later his hand came down on the man's shoulder. Thane spun him around, snatched the camera, and flung it down.

The man yelled and swung at Thane who ducked and raised his fists. "Damn you, that's a Nikon!" the man yelled as he swung again.

Thane side-stepped. "Pick up the pieces and go. Leave the lady alone, mister!"

A shrill whistle blasted the air and three policemen spilled out of the station.

Brett wanted a chasm to yawn open, a nice big hole where she could disappear and not be involved with Mr. T. Prescott. The smashed camera lay on the walk, male voices were raised in shouts while more policemen came outside. She wondered if she could quietly get out of Thane's car and walk away unnoticed. Let them put him away behind bars. At least her world might be safe!

She heard Thane's voice clearly say, "I'll sue the paper. . . ."

Groaning, she ran her hand across her aching temple. He threatened to sue the paper when he didn't have a job!

All heads turned toward her as the reporter clutched his smashed camera and gestured at the car. Her heart dropped. She wasn't going to escape. Why had she expected to when Thane was involved? A uniformed man approached the car and leaned down to look in the window at her.

From the back Manuel squawked, "Bastard! What legs!"

The policeman stared at the bird, nonplussed. Brett felt on fire with embarrassment and anger. "Officer, I'm sorry."

"We're taking Prescott in while we get this settled. He asked someone to tell you he might be a while."

"I'm coming." She twisted to look at Manuel. It might be too hot for the bird to stay in the car. She wanted to open the cage and throw the parrot into the street. Let him fly back to the jungle. Instead, she picked up the cage and climbed out of the car to follow the cluster of men. A mass of dark brown curls led the way as if the man owned the station.

As soon as she entered the lobby, a policeman turned to block her path.

"Sorry, lady, you'll have to wait here."

Thane paused, looking over the heads of the others, his manner as calm as a May morning. "I won't be long." His blue eyes settled on an officer. "I want to place a call to my lawyer, Mr. Harrison Atterbury, in Chicago."

Brett felt a shock. Even if she hadn't grown up around lawyers, she would have recognized the name of Harrison Atterbury. He didn't lose cases, and he cost an arm and two legs to hire. She blinked in surprise at Thane. An unemployed inventor hiring Harrison Atterbury? He'd said, "my lawyer." He already knew Atterbury. It didn't surprise her that he'd needed a lawyer in the past. The request had its effect on the others too. The officer's eyes had narrowed and suddenly he was calling Thane, "Mr. Prescott." The reporter's head had whipped around, his own eyes widening as he stared at Thane.

And she knew that whatever happened, Thane would come out in his usual unscathed manner, leaving devastation behind. Even though she didn't want her picture in the evening paper, she felt a surge of sympathy for the reporter.

She placed Manuel's cage in the corner. His beady eyes focused on her as she knelt down. "Not one word out of you, friend, or you'll be on someone's dinner table!" He ruffled his feathers and gave a squawk as she dropped the cover over his cage.

The men disappeared into an office and she sat down to wait. It wasn't twenty minutes before Thane reappeared around the corner. At the sight of him something punched all the breath out of her. His walk proclaimed he owned the world. His wide brow indicated his keen mind. His blue, blue eyes revealed his heart. And sent hers racing. Pity the others. She could imagine their faces, looking like Chicken Little when the sky fell. He strode over to her and she rose to her feet.

"I'll get Manuel," she said.

Thane's white teeth showed in a broad smile. "You're not going to ask if I'm on bond. If I'm to stand trial."

She took a deep breath. "I suspect the Shreveport Police Department is a hit-and-run victim, demolished by you."

He chuckled. His dark curls were in disarray, giving him a rakish look. "Don't sound so angry about it."

"You get to me sometimes."

"That's progress." His voice lowered to its sexy huskiness as he said, "I intend to get to you more than you can imagine!"

"Thane . . ." She felt so agitated, befuddled by him.

He smiled. "Let's go. I see smoke rising in your gray eyes again." He reached down to take the birdcage out of her hand, holding her arm as they walked toward the door.

"Where's the reporter?"

"Ed Grayson? I don't know. He's coming. Want to meet him?"

"Indeed not! Is my picture with Manuel going to be in the paper?"

"Nope." His dimple deepened. "Not unless you give Ed permission to take another."

"Well, I don't!"

"Grayson was disappointed, but he agreed it would be in everyone's best interests if no picture appeared."

"How'd you do it?"

He chuckled. "Don't look at me as if I just beat him to a pulp. He had Sergeant Thurgood and four other policemen with him."

As they walked toward the door, she caught his fresh, clean scent again and took a deep breath. "You're evading my question. I don't know how you do it! You see what I mean about a cyclone?"

As his dimple deepened, he touched her chin. "You're the one whose picture the photographer wanted, not me."

Aggravated, she said, "You haven't finished telling me about one calamity when another happens!"

She brushed against his chest as she went out the door. She was acutely aware of the slightest touch, of his presence at her side. As he followed, he said, "Your dad's fine. He's on his way to Caddo Lake now." They stepped out into the sunlight. Thane let the door swing shut, took her arm, then paused. Running his hand over his thick curls, he said, "Laurel, did you move my car?"

She stopped at the top of the wide steps and her gaze swept the curb. Only a police car and a black Ford were parked in front. She couldn't believe her eyes. Suddenly, her heart began a wild hammering that had occurred more and more often since Thane had entered her life. "It was right there."

"Honey," he drawled, "did you get out and leave the keys in my MG?"

The door opened behind them and the reporter emerged. One look at Thane and his gaze shifted.

Brett felt hot, then cold. Trembling started in her knees, working its way upward. "How could someone steal your car from in front of the police station?"

The reporter stopped with his foot hanging in midair off the top step. He turned. "Your car just got stolen?"

Ignoring the question, Thane rubbed his jaw with his blunt, tanned fingers. "I liked that little red MG. Ronnie helped me to select it."

Brett was horrified, stricken. It was her fault. Thane had jumped out and left her with the car, with the keys, and she had walked right off, leaving them behind. "Merciful heavens!"

"Merciful heavens is right," he said dryly, taking her arm. "We better report it."

"Holy Hannibal!" Ed Grayson snapped. "My camera's broken and here's a super story!" Suddenly he dashed ahead of them back into the building.

Brett couldn't move. She felt a tug on her arm and looked up at Thane. The sun behind him made a halo of his rich chestnut hair. He was gazing down at her, a questioning expression on his handsome features. A cyclone, a wizard, whatever he was, she couldn't take it! This was the last straw.

"Dammit!" she said, her voice dropping to the low, whispery tone that revealed her emotions. "Damn you, Thane Prescott!"

He blinked. Lines fanned from the corners of his eyes and his lips pursed. "What happened to 'merciful heavens!?"

"Dammit!"

"You leave my keys in the car and someone steals it and you get mad at *me*?" He couldn't keep the laughter out of his blue eyes and her rage heightened.

"My life was normal until yesterday. Until yesterday I didn't leave keys in cars. I didn't get my picture taken with weird birds for the daily paper! I didn't set skillets on fire!" She was trembling with fury. "I had a routine life. It was peaceful. Now I can't think! I can't do anything right!"

The dimple appeared, fueling her temper. The door opened again and Ed Grayson dashed across the lawn. Brett watched him briefly but her thoughts were elsewhere. "I can't eat. I can't sleep!"

Thane folded his arms around his chest and grinned.

"Don't you grin at me! You're going to stop raining on my parade, Thane Prescott! You're a Pied Piper and I've trailed along, straight in to disaster and disaster and disaster. My little brother's wearing your wild underwear, my father barely escaped arrest. . . ." She shook her fist at him.

Thane laughed. "Got it!" a man suddenly called

and they both looked down at the sidewalk. Ed Grayson was standing there with another man with a camera. Behind them at the curb was a car with the door open, the motor running.

Grayson waved. "I just wanted a story about your car getting stolen in front of the police station," he called, then ran toward the waiting car.

Brett gasped for breath. What had she done? She had actually shaken her fist at Thane, and in front of a photographer. Thane's eyes were dancing devilishly as he settled his hands on her shoulders.

"What is so damned funny?" she snapped.

"There go the strings off the package, Laurel. Pop, pop, pop! We'll get you unwrapped faster than I expected."

Suddenly her fury evaporated and she felt limp, dazed, in shock. What was the matter with her? "I've never, never lost my temper like that. That's the first time in my whole life I've shaken my fist at someone."

He dropped his arm around her shoulder, picked up Manuel, and headed for the door. "Did you good, honey. It was long overdue."

"Thane, people go through a whole lifetime without losing control like that."

They stepped inside the cool hall and Sergeant Thurgood turned to them.

"Sir, I want to report a theft," Thane said.

The sergeant straightened and another uniformed man turned to give his attention to Thane. "My car," he continued, "a red MG, was parked in front. When I jumped out after Grayson's camera, I left the keys in the car. The keys, my suitcase, my billfold . . ."

Brett stared at him. Why? Why had she become a patent attorney? Why hadn't she done something simple, and then Thane Prescott wouldn't have entered her life. His car had been stolen, along with his coat, his billfold! She had lost her temper in public, shaken her fist at him on the police station steps! She didn't know which ranked as the largest calamity, the biggest shock. Stricken, she listened to his deep voice as he said calmly, "Sir, I have a particular fondness for that little car. I hope we can get it back."

Both men moved swiftly. "You'll have to give us the license number and a description."

Thane turned to her. Talking to her as if she were on the injured list, he said, "Honey, why don't you take Manuel and sit down over there. I won't be long."

She did what he suggested. She moved woodenly to a chair and set the cage beside her. The cover slipped off, but she didn't give it a thought. She was numb. They should have raised hurricane warnings when Thane moved back to town. She should have barricaded her emotions before the onslaught. Now, she'd just have to ride out the storm. Her gaze drifted to Thane's broad shoulders, his long legs as he disappeared down the corridor with the policemen. Somewhere, she suspected, a thief was going to wish he had never laid eyes on a little red MG.

In a short time Thane returned, looking as in command as ever. He walked over to her. "I called and rented a car. They agreed to bring it here and I said we'd be out in front."

"You have a strange effect on people. They're all but bowing and scraping to you here."

"It's my natural charm."

"And your modesty."

"And my Clark Kent approach," he said with a grin.

"Don't step into a phone booth and reappear with a big "S" on your chest!"

"Ronnie's the one with the Superman outfit. I only have a gorilla suit."

With a chuckle he picked up the birdcage and took her arm. She wondered how he would pay for the car with his billfold gone, but she wasn't going to ask. She glanced at her watch, surprised to see the time. "I can't go to lunch now. I have an appointment in thirty minutes. I have to get to the office."

"All right, I'll get you a sandwich and you can eat in your office."

A shiny black Ford slid to a stop in front of the station and they climbed in. Thane deposited the driver at the Regency Hotel, stopped at a McDonald's to get sandwiches, then let Brett off at her office. As she climbed out, she turned to look at him. "You'll get your car back."

"You sound sure." Amusement flared in his eyes.

"The powers that be wouldn't dare cross you!"

"What about a luscious five-foot-seven bundle of gray eyes, silky black hair, and long legs?"

"Collision course every time!" She wanted to slam the door in his face. So she did.

As he drove away, she thought she heard him laughing. She entered the building, walked straight to her own office and closed the door. For a quarter of an hour she sat and stared into space, not even bothering to eat, her mind whirling over the morning's events. She was caught in the aftermath of another of Thane's storms.

She finally stirred when her client appeared, a nice, pale little man with a new type of airbrush.

After he left, the shock began to wear off. She spent the next hour working furiously on research about Thane's inventions. She felt desperate to finish the work with him, to get him out of her life. But around three she paused, dropping her pencil on the papers spread out on her desk, and stared at a paneled wall. Her thoughts returned to Ronnie, his wide, timid blue eyes. Ronnie needed playmates his own age. As fascinating as Thane was, the little boy should get out of the house, away from his father, and be with other children. He'd gotten along fine with Horace and that was two miracles right there. Horace wasn't a social person either, but it wasn't because of shyness. She remembered Ronnie's soft curls, his thin fingers twisting her hair.

She picked up a phone book and called the Caddo Parish school board to ask them about late enrollment, class size, the school in Thane's district. After she hung up, she gazed at the open book, then turned to private schools. Remembering the implacable thrust to Thane's firm jaw all the time she punched buttons, she called the closest school and jotted down notes.

In a short time she had contacted three private schools and had information on them. Carefully, she folded the paper and slipped it into her briefcase. She would confront Thane about the matter after dinner. Thane. She'd better polish her battle armor. His blue eyes danced in front of her. She hadn't known him twenty-four hours, yet he had rearranged her life! He called her Laurel, he'd stirred up so many memories, the first man since Wade . . . Remembering Thane's kiss caused something to knot inside her. Fires danced to life, burning hotly. His kisses . . . She forced her thoughts away from them. He had brought about some kind of transformation in her father. Even Horace had been switched out of his groove by Thane and Ronnie. Horace was so antisocial, yet suddenly he was willing to make friends with Ronnie. Thoughts of the tiger-striped underwear sent her back to work with a vengeance.

When she reached home, she could see from the drive that someone had lit the grill. She parked her car and walked around to the shaded backyard. Thane, dressed in tight jeans and a blue cotton short-sleeved shirt, was standing beside the smoking grill with Greg and Horace nearby. In spite of her lingering anger, her resolutions during the afternoon, her common sense, her heart jumped at the sight of Thane. His thick curls and blue eyes gave her a charge that nothing else could. As she approached, he waved a spatula over the grill.

"The fellows couldn't wait to eat, so I told them I'd feed them early. You and I'll eat later."

Was there a hidden promise in his words or an open threat to her peace? She crossed the yard to where Horace and Greg had spread out Thane's game on a wrought iron table on the patio. "Where's Ronnie?"

Horace glanced up. "Playing on my computer. Guess what? Mr. Prescott made up a neat new game for the computer."

"A veritable wizard," she said dryly and received a mocking glance from Thane. "Good. Horace, may I see you a minute?" She would settle the matter of the underwear as fast as possible.

He looked up, pushing black hair out of his eyes as he rose to his feet. "Brett, Laurel . . . Mr. Prescott calls you Laurel, doesn't he?"

"Yes."

"He said we could sleep in his yard in his tent tonight. I've never slept in a tent."

Addled, she stared at her younger brother. In his usual style, Thane had taken charge, giving the boys permission to go, leaving her alone with him

for the night. She wasn't sure she could handle a
whole night with Thane. She couldn't handle him
for five minutes. Her gaze drifted down her brother's lanky frame.

"Horace, you're wearing jeans!" Crisp, new blue
jeans hung on his bony hips.

He grinned. "Mr. Prescott wants us to help him
with his house tomorrow. He said I'd need some
jeans."

While he talked he moved closer. A whiff of enticing aftershave reached her and she received
another shock. "Horace! You're—" She stopped
abruptly, biting her lip.

Horace asked, "What were you going to say?"
while Thane studied her curiously.

"Let's go in the kitchen," she said to her brother.

"Yeah. Just a minute, Greg."

Thane moved back to the grill and Brett led the
way. As soon as the door closed behind them, she
turned around. "Horace, this morning Mr. Prescott couldn't find his underwear."

Horace's face turned bright pink and his hazel
eyes shifted to the window. "He talked to me about
it. He wasn't mad."

"And now you're wearing his aftershave! You
don't even shave! Did you ask if you could?"

Horace jammed his hands in his pockets and
shuffled his feet. "Uh, no."

"Look here, you have to stay out of his things.
You know better than to do that. Talk about a little
kid getting into *your* room!"

"Aww . . ."

A light rap sounded and the door opened. Thane
thrust his head into the room, then entered, his
blue eyes darting swiftly from Brett to Horace.
"Excuse me, do I need some hamburger buns or to
rescue anyone?"

Horace's thin chest expanded as he took a deep breath. "Mr. Prescott, may I use your aftershave?"

"Sure, Horace." His blue eyes became thoughtful. Too damn thoughtful and Brett felt a nervous prickle.

Thane picked up a package of buns and Horace started toward the door. He hesitated, then asked, "Brett, uh, Laurel, how'd you know I have on Mr. Prescott's aftershave?"

With a satisfied smirk, Thane turned back to her. She felt the blush starting. "I just guessed!" she snapped and rushed into the hall, hearing a deep chuckle behind her.

She hurried to her room to soak in a tub and try to forget everything, especially Mr. T. Prescott. Which was about as easy as roller-skating through the Grand Canyon. There were rocks in her path. Boulders. Blue eyes, a wicked dimple, soft curly hair. It was impossible to forget he was waiting for her downstairs. She dressed carefully in a brown skirt and a simple white oxford cloth shirt. She couldn't look plainer. With a vengeance she combed her hair up and put twice as many pins in the bun, reminding herself to keep his big fingers out of her hair, but the mere thought made her turn to jelly inside.

A train whistle shrieked and she paused. The Pied Piper's tune. It called her heart, beckoning her to follow.

With a determined lift to her chin, she went downstairs. When she stepped outside, only Ronnie was in sight. The top of the grill was down and everything was neatly arranged with the table covered by a red tablecloth and set for two. Ronnie stood up when she entered.

"Dad took the boys to show them how to run the train. He said for me to wait and come with you."

"Good." Ronnie was so solemn, she longed to make him smile. She started toward the front.

"Mrs. Fortier, my Dad showed me a shortcut. Come on this way." She followed him, moving faster to catch up and walk beside him.

They cut across their backyard, through the Waters' backyard, then the Eastmans' until they faced a high wooden fence. Without hesitation Ronnie walked to a small mimosa, stepped on a low branch, reached up, and hoisted himself to the top of the fence. He looked down at her. "Can you climb up here?"

The first tinge of aggravation began to stir. Brett put her foot on the branch, grasped the top of the rough boards and hauled herself up to sit easily on the fence. Her back was to Thane's yard and she faced someone else's home. As she watched the back door opened and a man emerged from the house and stared at her.

Embarrassment flooded her. How could she explain why she was sitting on his fence? She smiled and waved. From behind, strong hands closed around her waist and she was lifted down, pulled into Thane's arms, held against his warm chest. Gazing into his blue eyes, she forgot everything else momentarily.

When Thane smiled, she had to respond, to smile in return. "Hi, Laurel," he said.

The shrill toot of the train jarred her senses. "You get me into more predicaments. Your neighbor must've wondered what I was doing on his fence."

"I'd be glad to see you on mine any day. It's my fence and not his. Just a minute." He set her on the ground and she saw he was standing on a large rock. He waved and called over the fence, "Hi, Ted. You and Betty want to join us?

While the men conversed, Brett turned to see the miniature train chugging slowly around the yard. A puff of smoke came from the smokestack. With an engineer's cap on his head and a big grin on his face, Horace sat at the controls. Behind him in the next open car rode Greg. Behind Greg were four more empty cars and a red caboose. Horace slowed as Thane turned from the fence and walked Brett over to the train. "Hop on board," Horace said.

Ronnie scrambled on. Thane swung his long legs over the side, then lifted Brett in easily. "Let's take a turn before we go back to your house. I showed Horace how to run it. We'll leave them in a minute."

He seated her and dropped his arm around her. Ronnie sat in the car in front of them and he turned to grin at them before Horace started the train again.

Enjoying the breeze in the shaded yard, she rode in the train with the Pied Piper's arm around her. Held against his shoulder, she glanced up at him, at his fine features, his thick curls blowing in the wind. She wondered about him. What a strange and marvelous man he was—sensitive, imaginative, dynamic. Maybe a little too dynamic. Pure trouble. A strange, forlorn feeling touched her, a hollow feeling of sorrow. She wasn't the woman for a man like Thane, no matter how much she might secretly want to be.

They rode four turns around the yard before Thane called to Horace to stop. He swung Brett out, climbed out himself, then gave some final instructions to Horace. As the train chugged away, the boys waved. Thane looked at her. "Ready?"

"Do I have to scale the fence again?"

He grinned. "Rather take the long way home?"

"I think so, yes."

He held her hand and they walked around the

block, back to her house. With each step she was aware of his nearness, of his hand holding hers. Excitement radiated from his large body and charged through her, making her intensely aware of every moment. When they reached her backyard, she heard the phone and hurried inside.

It was a call for Thane. While he talked, she discovered that he'd already made a large tossed salad, that two potatoes were baking in the oven, and that two steaks were ready for the grill.

He replaced the phone and turned to face her. "They found my car."

"I knew they would. Is it all right?"

A muscle twitched, indicating a grin was lurking nearby. "The thief was flagged down for speeding and when the police gave chase, he lost control of the car. He jumped out and ran, leaving it in a field. No harm done."

No harm done. She thought about her explosion on the steps of the police station.

Tilting her chin up, he lost the battle with a grin. "Shall I put on a helmet and asbestos coat? I see smoke rising."

"No harm done," she repeated. Just his finger on her chin had altered her heartbeat. "You did it again."

"There's just one area where I definitely want to get my way."

"Is that so?" Her heartbeat suffered another setback.

His eyebrow raised at a rakish angle and his blue eyes developed a challenging male look. "And I will have my way. That, my lovely, is a promise."

Her heartbeat gave up the ghost and stopped. For whole seconds it seemed. Her voice was breathless. "I wish you wouldn't do that."

"The hell you do," he said huskily. "I can see the

fight in your eyes. Give in. Let the woman in you win. Come on out into the world again, Laurel. Don't be afraid to give life a try."

She felt shaky and her voice wouldn't rise beyond a husky depth. She said, "Don't be ridiculous!" as she turned away quickly.

There was a moment's silence, then he said, "Come sit down while I cook dinner."

Shaken, she reached for two wine glasses. "I think it's supposed to be the other way around since you're the guest."

"I had more time to get dinner ready today, and Harriet showed me where things are."

A twinge of fear shook Brett. She paused, setting the glasses on the counter. "Showed you where things are? Did she fill you in on family history too?" She held her breath, waiting for his answer.

While he poured the burgundy, he said, "Matter of fact, she did. She said you had a whirlwind courtship and marriage, moved to San Diego with your young man and stayed for a year after his death before you came home to live." His eyes met hers. "She said the family didn't see anything of you during the year you lived in San Diego. That you stayed with his folks."

A knot formed in the pit of her stomach. While she filled two tumblers with ice water, she said, "That's right. Harriet has you right up to date."

She saw the questions burning in his blue eyes as he held the door open for her. She didn't want to be quizzed about the past, not by a wizard with a bag of tricks, so she brushed past him without looking at him. His familiar aftershave assailed her, that enticing scent that would remind her forever of Thane. In the shade on the patio, she sat down while he worked, knowing he was watching her with curiosity. Within a few minutes he joined her.

There didn't seem to be an appropriate time, an opening, to talk to him about Ronnie. During dinner and afterward, talk was light, inconsequential as they learned about each other's past. It was too light. She felt as if she were in the calm before the storm, as if unseen clouds were gathering in the chair beside her. Thane met everything head-on and she suspected another emotional clash was coming, yet he sat quietly and talked about college, growing up, moving away. The only thing that wasn't inconsequential was his presence. His briefly, lightly touching her arm, brushing her knee, moving to sit close, stroking the nape of her neck.

Every second she became more nervous. She was acutely aware of the fiery feel of his fingers, his eyes, his long body so close to her. His short-sleeved shirt left his tanned, muscular arms bare and she remembered how they had felt around her waist, how easily he had swung her down off the fence. She studied the watch on his wrist. It was flat and gold without numbers, a Piaget and expensive. Questions sprang to her mind about him, but there was something else more important. She waged a mental battle with herself and decided to bring up the subject of Ronnie's schooling at a more propitious moment. She wanted to discuss Ronnie, but such an emotional topic would be deeply personal and she didn't want to take the risk of Thane asking about her own life. Since when had she become such a coward?

When the stars blinked into sight, a chill settled on the patio, yet she didn't want to go inside, into the intimacy of the house.

Remembering how swiftly he had blocked her exit

from the kitchen the night before, her pulse speeded up. She rose to her feet in a fluid movement and walked to the door, putting space and furniture between them before she announced casually, "Thane, I brought some reading home and it's been a long day. If you'll excuse me, I think I'll turn in."

"Sure, Laurel. 'Night."

Just like that. So damned simple. There wasn't one simple, easy thing about Mr. T. Prescott. She entered the kitchen, switching on the light over the sink, then headed upstairs to her room. She started to undress, then decided to wait a while and settled at her desk to work. She read the same line five times before she realized she was tense, listening for Thane to come upstairs.

Aggravated that he was so unpredictable, she tried again to concentrate. In a few minutes she gave it up as useless.

She gritted her teeth, feeling a captive in her own home. Her wide gray eyes met her reflection in the mirror. Captive of what? She looked around the room, seeing the furnishings with Thane's eyes. Her bedroom was plain and bare, as devoid of pictures or knick-knacks as the rest of the house. The bed with its square mahogany headboard had a white quilted spread. The white curtains blending with the white walls, creating a harmless, sterile atmosphere. There was a mahogany mirror, her desk, one bedside table with a lamp and a clock. Nothing else. The dresser held two lamps, a mirrored tray, and one bottle of perfume. The room was the way she wanted it. There were no memories to torment her, no past to cling to.

Clamping her jaw down until it ached, she tried again to work. Why didn't he come? It was cold outside without a sweater. With his boots, he couldn't tiptoe inside noiselessly. She remembered asking him if he ever did anything quietly and his suggestive, silly answer, his twinkling eyes as he studied the four-poster bed.

Angrily, she shoved the papers into her briefcase, cleaned off her desk and undressed, bathing again just to kill time. After the bath she dressed in the white cotton gown, took down her hair, and brushed it with a vengeance. What was he doing? She hadn't heard a sound. The evening was so uncharacteristic of him, the first peaceful few hours since she met him in his front yard on Thursday. She turned down the bed, shut off the light, and crossed to the window to look for him on the patio.

The light tap on the door behind her made her jump and gasp with shock. She whirled and stared wide-eyed at the door. She couldn't speak, couldn't summon her voice. Realizing she had let her worries work her into a dither, she shook her fist at the door. "What now?" she snapped.

"I'd like to talk to you." Did she hear laughter?

She couldn't breathe. He surely wouldn't come in if she said no. But then, how could she guess anything he might do? "No," she whispered, then spoke more firmly. "Not on your life!"

There was silence. Total silence. She waited and waited before climbing into bed. Finally, she decided he had gone to his room. She lay stiffly in the darkness, knowing that sleep was impossible, fighting the knowledge that Thane was only a room away, that big, powerful body . . . She groaned and squeezed her eyes shut.

The shrill wail of an alarm cut through the silence and her eyes flew open.

Seven

She blinked and sat up. It was one of their fire alarms. Something was on fire downstairs! "Oh my lord," she whispered, tossing back the covers. He'd already burned down his own house, what now?

She raced down the steps. The alarm was in the kitchen and when she turned down the hall toward it, she could see a light glowing from the doorway.

She dashed into the kitchen. It was empty. She whirled around and her heart stopped.

Thane stood under the alarm, a flaming cigarette lighter in his hand. He clicked it shut and lowered his arm, smiling at her below hooded eyes while silence enveloped them.

Stunned, she stared at him as fury swept over her. One big hand was hooked into his wide brown leather belt. He had unbuttoned the blue shirt, revealing his tanned, furred chest. A soft light glowed behind him over the counter, framing his broad shoulders, and mass of curls.

His blue eyes met hers full force, stirring a tempest, setting everything inside her aflutter. Her heart was thudding against her ribs as her instinct for self-preservation surfaced.

"Damn you! Why didn't you just barge into my room?"

"You didn't invite me in."

She fought another urge to shake her fist at him. "Do you know what you just did to me? I thought the house was on fire! That we had an emergency."

"We do," he drawled in husky tones. Slowly, his gaze lowered over her nightgown, drifting down the shapeless white cotton that buttoned to her chin, covered her to her wrists and toes, and she felt as if it had vanished beneath his scrutiny.

She quivered, caught in a swirl of emotions. Anger changed to fear and fear changed to something she didn't want to acknowledge. He straightened and started toward her.

She wanted away from him more than anything else. Pure, raw emotion took control of her and she reacted blindly, without thinking. Before he'd taken two steps she was halfway out the door.

He caught her easily, his strong arms banding aorund her waist. "Laurel, honey . . ."

"I don't want to talk. I don't want you to probe into my life." She twisted, struggling futilely, her dark hair flying over her shoulders as her head thrashed.

He kissed her thoat, his warm lips trailing up to her ear, across her cheek as her protest became fainter and fainter.

His enticing scent surrounded her, his warm breath smelled of mint. His chest was so solid, so secure. Her balled fists uncurled, flattening out, her fingers spread against his chest, slid beneath his open shirt to rest on the soft mat of curls.

His mouth touched hers, taking her lips, parting them to his thrusting tongue.

Golden hot explosions started, a profound reaction bursting through her in shock waves, making her tremble, frightening her more than anything had for so long. She gathered her strength, tearing her lips from his. "Can't you understand? I don't want you to kiss me!"

She couldn't push away his implacable arms of steel. Gasping, she looked up at him. His blue eyes were smoldering. "What are you afraid of, Laurel?" he asked bluntly.

Her breast heaved as she tried to get her breath. Thane Prescott was trouble! His life was not orderly, quiet, and sane; he was too much of a shock to her settled world. She didn't want to let go of her protective barriers.

He was waiting and she realized he would stand there until dawn if he had to, until she answered him. She couldn't fight his strength and she hated him for it, for forcing her to remember.

"I don't want to hurt anymore!" she cried. "When I lost Wade, it hurt so damn much, I'd rather be half alive than go through agony like that again. Don't make me dredge it all up. . . ."

Her throat burned and tears threatened. Fiercely, she blinked them back. "Now, are you satisfied?"

"You're fighting tears."

"That's right! I'm fighting because I've shed enough to fill an ocean! Now you have your confession, you know my secrets."

He shook his head. "That's not all."

"Not all!" Terrified, she didn't want him to probe and push until she had to face it all again, the miscarriage in her fifth month, the agony of loss. "You've caused enough pain." The words were torn from her. "I've made a life for myself!" Suddenly the words came faster, tumbling out in a breathless rush. "It may not be anything great, but it's peaceful. Don't destroy it! Don't smash it, Thane."

His thick-lashed eyes aimed steadfastly at her, stabbing into her relentlessly. A husky, sensuous drawl enveloped her as strongly as his arms. "I won't let you go, babe. We're halfway home. . . ." His arms tightened. "You know, I warned you I'm going to kiss you until you answer all my questions."

His words scared her even while they set her on fire. He crushed her to his chest, his mouth taking command in a primitive kiss that drove all thought out of her mind. Deep into her mouth, into her soul, he explored, demanding from her a response that began to burn to life, then to roar out of control. Fire raged between them, sent waves of searing heat that forged a chain of need. Her arms slipped around his neck, her body fitted closer to his strong male length.

Longing came shuddering to life, wracking her as she fought it and lost. She tumbled over a brink, falling with dizzying speed into a flaming abyss of desire. Her fingers wound in Thane's hair, crushing the soft curls while her hips thrust against his hard loins, his maleness.

"That's it, babe!" he whispered hoarsely as his mouth found her ear. "Let go, honey, give! There's so much woman in you!"

"No," she whispered, her eyes still closed. "Leave me alone, please." But even as she spoke her head moved against his shoulder and she kissed the flesh that stretched tautly over his collarbone.

"Inside you there's a woman of love and life and laughter." He rained kisses, hot and moist, over skin that sprang to life beneath his touch.

His big fingers fumbled with the buttons at the throat of her nightgown while his lips returned to hers to stop a protest, to drown her resistance. He pushed away the thick cotton, his warm palm resting on her collarbone, his fingers drifting down over her breast.

Agony, joy, rippled in her. She couldn't withstand his caresses.

His fingertips brushed the slope of her breast and she gasped. His hand circled, cupped her heated, throbbing flesh. His thumb, warm and callused, scraped across an aching nipple, making her writhe in torment.

"Laurel," he breathed in ragged tones, his hand trembling as he held her.

When she felt his tremor, her eyes flew open. Dark curls fell over his forehead. With his eyes closed, his thick lashes shadowed his cheeks. He drew a deep, shuddering breath and leaned down to kiss her breast, to touch and explore her eager, pink-tipped flesh.

He was caught and held in the same magic spell as she. Sorcery wove an enchantment. She wanted this big man so desperately, but she knew if she gave herself to him physically, she would give her heart too. She was afraid of where that commitment might lead. Thane was overwhelming. She couldn't cope with his powerful, demanding maleness. The old inadequacies rose to haunt her, to torment her. She wasn't the woman he thought she was, and he rushed her too swiftly toward . . . Her mind blanked, then met the realization squarely. He rushed her toward emotional involvement. She wasn't ready yet. Not at all. No matter how much her body cried out for him, her emotions weren't ready for a man again.

A violent quivering began inside, shaking her so strongly that he noticed. His lashes raised and his blue eyes focused, then narrowed on her.

"I can't fight your strength," she said breathlessly. "But there'll be a point beyond which you'll have to use force. I can go so far and no farther."

His eyes cut into her heart. "Why? What is it, honey?" He drew a ragged breath. "After all these years are you so in love with him you can't lead a normal life? Don't you know I understand the loss, the pain? Laurel, I've been through it."

She shook her head. She couldn't talk, but he waited, finally tilting her chin up. His voice was puzzled, tender. "I haven't seen a picture of him anywhere in this house. It's something else, isn't it?"

Her eyes flew open. "Yes! And I know you well enough to know that you're the one who wouldn't take an affair lightly. You wouldn't let me withhold anything. Yet, I can't give you enough. And I can't cope with the way you live. Everywhere you go, there's a storm of trouble! I'm not ready for that."

"Oh lord, Laurel . . ." His arms tightened, but she resisted.

"You can keep on," she said firmly, "but sooner or later, there will come a point where I have to stop. I'm not a tease; I'm warning you now. I won't let you make love to me because I'll get hurt too badly."

"This won't hurt you," he whispered and leaned down to kiss her, but she turned her head.

His blue eyes leveled on her, probed, and his arms loosened. "Laurel, I won't give you up. When your big gray eyes focus on me, something spectacular happens between us. To me—and to you."

Her heart was pounding against her ribs. She wasn't conscious of how she looked to him, her lips rosy from his kiss, her prim nightgown unbuttoned, the collar pushed aside to reveal the soft curve of her breast, her cloud of raven hair cascading over her shoulders to her waist, her devastated eyes, forlorn yet still smoldering with leashed passion. His voice was a deep rasp. "I'll stop now, but I won't let you out of my life."

Shaken, she drew a sharp breath and left, climbing the stairs without looking back, his words engraved in her mind. When she reached her room she closed the door and sat down at the desk, clinging to it as if it were a lifesaver.

How could she settle into her dull, routine, ordinary life again and forget him? How could she have an affair with him? He was too full of life, too demanding, too eccentric.

She dropped her head into her hands and closed her eyes. Long into the night her logical lawyer's mind debated the arguments. She rose and crossed to the window to gaze into the darkness outside. There were three choices—get him out of her life; have an affair; or, if it led so far, marry him. All three were disasters.

She stared into the dark yard, her throbbing head resting against the cold, smooth pane. Would she ever be the same? When he moved out, she wouldn't have to see him again except when they discussed his patents, but was that what she really wanted? She had known him such a short time, yet she couldn't imagine life without him.

Alternative two, an affair . . . She sighed. When it ended, Thane's absence would be as bad as losing Wade, maybe worse. With Wade she had been so young, it had happened so swiftly that it had an unreal, dreamlike quality. It wouldn't be that way now, not with Thane. An affair was out.

That left the third alternative, something *he* might not want. Marriage. Impossible! She was an orderly person. She lived with routine and reason. With Thane she would never know what to expect.

And she might not be able to have children. Too clearly, she could remember Dr. Patterson's prognosis, that the chance she could have a normal pregnancy was slim. With many men her ability to have children wouldn't matter, but with Thane it would. He loved Ronnie. He was just the kind of man who would want more children. She couldn't bear to deny him a large family.

The best choice of the three was to stay away from him. When she faced that fact, she felt desolate. He called her Laurel, and she was beginning to like that. He'd brought zest, fun, excitement into her life. He exuded an overpowering maleness. His bedroom eyes with their curly lashes; his thick soft brown curls; that long, hard, muscular body, so fit, so enticing . . . She stopped as her train of thought led too easily to thinking about his kisses, the marvelous feeling of his arms around her, the magic of his blue, blue eyes. She turned to look at the clock and was shocked to see it was a few minutes after two in the morning. She wondered if Thane could sleep. Probably without effort.

She stretched out on the bed, turned out the light, and stared at the ceiling. Memory of Thane's passionate kisses, his hands drifting lightly over her, tormented her and she groaned, tossing and turning in bed. The minutes crept past. Half-past two. Suddenly something exploded. A bang reverberated through the house.

She sat up, frowning at the door. What now? She climbed out of bed and peered into the hall. It, like the rest of the house, was dark. Her heart began to hammer. Switching on the hall lights, she walked to his door. "Thane!"

There was silence. Grimly, she looked at the door. Was it another one of his tricks or some real calamity? The explosion had been real enough. "Thane!"

Still only silence. Her nerves grew taut. What was he doing? She knocked. "Thane!"

Cautiously, she opened the door. Light from the hall spilled into the darkened room, slicing over the rumpled bed, cutting a bright swath across the floor. Thane was lying on the floor, clad only in jeans, his chest and feet bare. Her heart jumped to her throat as she rushed to kneel down beside him. His lashes fluttered.

"What on earth happened?" she asked.

His lashes raised and he stared at her blankly.

"Are you all right? What happened?"

He didn't answer and her fright increased. Nearby, she saw a blackened electrical socket in the wall with a black extension cord plugged into it. *"Are you all right?"*

He just stared at her. She placed her ear against his warm, bare chest, her hair spreading over his shoulders and stomach as she listened to his racing heart. "Thane . . ."

His arms closed around her tightly, pulling her down against him. She gasped and tried to turn away but his hand cupped the back of her head, pulling her the remaining few inches to kiss her. His mouth touched hers and she felt her own explosion, a jolt that rocked her and set her heart pounding. Caught offguard, she yielded, one shock following another. His mouth opened hers; his tongue sent her senses reeling, blotting out reality. She returned his kiss and her heart responded like a bird on a cloudless day, soaring through space, rising on unseen currents. Her fingers slipped across the extraordinary expanse of his shoulders to touch his warm throat, then drifted up to brush against his soft curls, his ears.

Grasping her hips, he shifted her along his length. It had been so long since she had been loved, since she had felt a man's hard body against her. The sensations were heady, so perfect. His hand started at her neck and trailed across her shoulder blades, down her back, over the soft curve of her buttocks to her legs. The surging current caused by his caresses stormed her senses, made her thrust her hips against him, drove her to awareness of what was happening. In one swift movement she rolled away and stood up. Trembling, gasping for breath she stood over him.

"That was a low, cheap trick!"

His blue eyes were smoldering, making her want to tumble back down into his tanned, muscled arms. His broad chest expanded as he breathed deeply. "What was?"

"To kiss me like that!" He looked so damned handsome. She was burning inside, and the blaze was growing as she looked at him stretched on the floor, his broad coppery chest, his lips faintly pink from their kisses.

"I just had the stuffing shocked out of me!"

"You did that to get me in here, just like you set off the fire alarm!"

His dimple appeared. "I didn't give myself an electrical shock, blow the lights, burn my hand, to get your attention. You're working yourself into a snit while I'm burned and hurt."

Startled, she studied him. "Are you really?"

"A little." He sat up.

"Where?"

He grinned at her. "You won't calm down until I produce burned fingers, a bleeding wound, or—"

"Oh, for heaven's sake! Where are you hurt?"

He held out his hand and his fingers were covered with black. "I burned my fingers."

"Oh! I'm sorry!" He kept her in such a turmoil, she never knew what to expect. "Let me get something for that." She rushed to her bathroom, rummaged in the cabinet, and returned with an ointment. He still sat on the floor, his arms locked around his knees, his head on his arm.

"Thane, are you all right?"

He raised his head. "Just shaky. I thought I'd sit here a minute." His eyes twinkled. "I don't know if it's from shock or from your kiss."

Trying to ignore her fluttery reaction, she said, "Give me your hand. This is for burns." She sat down cross-legged beside him, her gown billowing around her. She held his hand on her knee, intensely aware of his warmth through the layer of cotton.

While she rubbed ointment gently on his fingers, she said, "I'm sorry. I never know what you're up to." She smoothed the gooey salve over his index finger, where a blister was already rising. "Do you always stay up this late."

"No." The hungry, aching note in his voice told her why he had been awake. Startled, she looked up to meet his sexy eyes. They captured her gaze, holding her so she couldn't look away. "I couldn't sleep, so I decided to work on a toy." His voice was husky. "Have you been asleep?"

She wanted to say yes, to stop what was happening between them before she lost control of her emotions, but she couldn't. "No, I couldn't sleep either."

He lifted a strand of hair away from her face. "You're lovely."

Her pleasurable reactions to him escalated. She was aware of the charged air, of every inch of his massive bare chest, his long legs, his big hands. "Sit still so I can do this." She tried to be firm, all business. She tried to concentrate on his hand. She tried to keep her voice from sounding breathless. She really tried. And failed completely.

He sounded faintly amused. "I blew a fuse. I'll throw the switch if you'll tell me where the box is."

"In the utility room. Your heart was racing. Do you feel better now?"

"Want to check again and see if it's still beating?" he asked, smiling cockily.

"Sure thing." Her fingers closed around his wrist.

"Chicken."

"But safe."

"Since when is safe fun?"

"Let me finish doctoring." Seeing the impudent glint in his eyes, she concentrated on his index finger, studying the roughened skin. Something was bothering her and she finally asked, "Thane, how did your house catch on fire?"

"I had a cauldron full of toadstools boiling and they blew up."

Startled, she looked up, then clamped her jaw closed. He laughed. "You think I set it on fire, don't you?"

"I ought to be beyond shock by now."

"Well to put your mind at ease, I didn't set my house on fire. There was a short in the wiring in the attic and the fire started while Ronnie and I were downstairs watching television."

She couldn't imagine Thane doing anything as ordinary as watching television. She tilted her head and regarded him intently. "What were your parents like?"

"Just plain people. My dad was a nice guy. He liked to fish, read. He always said to enjoy life, it was too short."

It was becoming more and more of an effort to

keep from looking at his broad chest, to keep from reaching out to touch the mat of curls. She noticed again the scar on the underside of his arms, the rough white line running up to his armpit, cutting across his smooth coppery skin. "Do you have brothers or sisters?"

"No. Just me."

"What about your mother? How did she cope with you?"

He grinned. "She kept house, went to her bridge club, and wrote poetry. I think most of the time she was in her own world with her mind on her poems. When I wrecked my motorcycle, I called her from the emergency room at the hospital. I told her I'd totaled the cycle and the first thing she asked was whether I wanted cauliflower or corn on the cob for dinner. I guess she thought if I could call, I was all right."

"Were you all right?"

"I broke my arm and skinned off half my hide." He twisted slightly to thrust his hip toward her. "I have a scar here." He patted his hip. "Want to see?"

"No!"

He laughed, then raised a brow and asked, "Why couldn't you sleep?"

She drew a sharp breath. His eyes were boring into her like a drill, cutting through layers of resistance. She straightened, her fingers holding his wrist on her knee.

"I was thinking about you. . . ."

"Laurel." His deep voice strummed her raw nerves.

Hastily, working up her courage, she added, "And I was worrying about Ronnie."

"Ronnie?"

She rushed into the subject, talking rapidly.

"Have you visited any schools here, talked with any teachers?"

"No." He let out a long breath. The blue depths changed, became as hard as a glacier.

"You just decided without looking into it that Ronnie should stay home?"

He pulled his knees up, wrapping his arms around his legs again, his face unreadable. "That's right. I know what my son needs. He's had problems."

"Maybe he's had problems, but don't compound them!" She was into the subject now and she laid her thoughts bare to him. "He's so little and solemn. Look at him with Horace. He's having a good time here."

"Which just goes to show you that he'll adjust next year when he goes back to school."

His jaw thrust forward slightly. She longed to reach up and push the dark curls off his forehead, to smooth his hair back and feel its silky softness against her hand. "After a year alone with only you, he may not." She hated to say it, but she couldn't forget Ronnie's timid gaze when they were introduced.

Thane shifted to rest his elbows on his knees. He rubbed his large fingers over his curls and she felt terrible, but couldn't shake the conviction that Ronnie would be better off if Thane put him in school. The light from the hall lit the room dimly, giving a burnished look to Thane's skin. With each passing minute she was more acutely conscious of his body, his bare chest, his feet just inches from her legs. She wanted to touch him so badly!

As he raised his head, his prominent cheekbones were highlighted while his cheeks were shadowy and dark. The thick fringe of his lashes was dark and curling around his eyes, eyes filled with the pain she had caused.

"You know Ronnie needs other children," she said.

Turning his burned hand to examine his fingers, he said, "This past year's been so hard on him and . . . we were practically strangers. I'm an engineer and I traveled a lot. . . ."

"What did you do when you worked?"

He smiled. "I still work, Laurel, I just work at inventing toys." His voice hardened as he added, "I had a construction company."

She mulled over what he'd said. It was easy to imagine him in construction, but she was surprised when he said he'd had his own company. "I don't mean to pry into your affairs. I'm just interested in Ronnie."

His lashes swept up and his gaze rested on her, making her draw a long, deep breath. His blue eyes were holding her captive again. He took the ointment from her hands and her heart wobbled crazily.

"You aren't interfering," he said. "I appreciate your concern. I just think I know what's best." His strong arms reached out to enfold her. He pulled her into his lap, holding her against his chest, and she couldn't say no. His husky voice had shattered her train of thought.

How could she talk with his lips inches away? She felt as if she were drowning in deep blue pools that were blanking out her thoughts.

"You're trying to sidetrack me," she protested faintly, "to get me off the subject."

"Trying?" He kissed her throat, starting a throbbing in her pulse.

"Thane." She placed her hands on both sides of his face and raised his head. Oh, lord, it was difficult to look at his mouth, his eyes, and think about anything else! While she studied his face, his well-shaped mouth, his slightly thrusting lower lip, her worries drifted away like smoke.

He brushed a long strand of hair from her face. His fingers caught more silky strands, smoothing them down as his knuckles slipped over her shoulder, her collarbone, down to the soft fullness of her breast. She caught his hand, holding it against her while her heart throbbed and her skin burned where he touched her.

His dark head lowered and his mouth found hers. A touch of velvet lips—soft yet firm—a tongue-tip—hot, seeking—then his mouth settled on hers, opening hers to take her sweetness, to stir her to life. He shifted, his lips trailing to her ear, his breath coming fast and heated. "Let go, Laurel. Come on, honey, life's waiting. I want your fire, your warmth. Laurel . . ." he whispered. Her body responded but still her heart held back. She was afraid, she wasn't the woman for him. But even as she repeated these arguments to herself, they became no more than fleeting clouds of fog drifting before the noonday sun, a sun whose golden rays demolished every ghostly tendril in its fiery orange heat.

His head lowered, his mouth seeking hers as his fingers pushed away her gown. He cupped her full breast in his big, capable hand. His lips trailed along her throat while his fingers fell oh, so delicately, so gently, like spindrift over a seawall, across her quivering willing flesh.

Her heart seemed to stop. Between her legs, low in her body, longing leaped to life, spreading a heated yearning that made her forget fear and logic. Radiating within her was a need that waved a magic wand, banishing the world and leaving only one magnificent man. With great effort she focused on his clear blue eyes. He looked deeply into her own eyes, probing as he caressed the taunt peaks of her breast, and he saw his answer.

"Laurel," he murmured and pulled her to him to bury his face in her throat, in her soft cloud of night-black hair. He kissed her passionately, a devouring kiss that burned her thoughts to oblivion. She barely noticed when he lowered her to the floor. He stretched his body along hers. His thigh nudged her legs apart and slid into the warmth between them, an insistent pressure that made her gasp and writhe and lose control. Reason and fear had held her, but Thane's hands and lips overrode the barriers. He undressed her, flinging away the gown. His own clothes were cast aside carelessly, revealing a superb male, bronzed, incredibly big and strong. Holding his powerful body in check, he loved her patiently. His hands explored her with the sweetness of warm honey, building such a need in her that she quivered and shook in his arms. She clung to him, to his strength, to his hard shoulders, responding to each stroke, each sensuous arousal.

Breathless, her heart hammering, she wound her arms around his neck and closed her eyes. The world spiraled dizzily as he swung her up and onto the bed, shoving aside tools that clattered to the floor.

She didn't care. She was beyond anything but her need for Thane. She stroked a stomach as flat and hard as burnished bronze and heard him gasp, felt him shudder when her fingers trailed over his hair-roughened thighs.

His fingers moved to the feminine warmth between her legs, touching, exploring, then stroking until she flung her arms around his shoulders while she writhed and arched against him. As he aroused her to a delirious peak of longing, her fingers bit into his flesh and she cried his name over and over before he hushed her with his mouth.

Finally, his weight shifted. He moved between her legs, lowering himself so slowly, so tantalizingly, that she cried his name softly and thrust her hips upward impatiently, her long legs holding him.

"Thane!"

"That's it, babe. That's my girl!" he whispered hoarsely. "Now, Laurel . . . oh, lord, how I want you. I want you. . . ."

She felt his thrusting heated warmth enter to awaken the deeply passionate woman in her. For one fleeting second she realized what she was doing. For one millisecond of a moment she wondered if she had committed the greatest folly of her life. Then he moved within her and all she knew was desire for Thane.

His hard maleness, his big body, his deliberate control carried her into a world of sensation, of ecstasy and rapture that were brilliant hues of a sensuous rainbow of feeling. Her need escalated; passion became frenzy until his control burned away and they were both in orbit, moving in unison to a shuddering climax before they dropped to earth and reality.

She lay beneath him, heated, damp, striving for breath, her legs and arms entwined with his. With effort she raised her lashes and drifted into his eyes, the blue wizardry that had worked its magic spell, that had enchanted her and won and bound to him forever some part of her heart.

She couldn't talk. She didn't want to break the spell, to leave enchantment. She knew she had crossed a boundary into trouble, but for the moment she didn't want to examine the new territory, the new plane of their relationship. She would just relish the strong arms and marvelous, solid body that seemed to protect her from all threats.

Thane pulled up the sheet, settling her against his chest, holding her to his heart while his hand stroked her hair. She traced his jaw with her finger, running her fingertip over the bristly skin, then up to his ear and into his silky curls.

"Laurel." His voice was a rumble, a deep, male sound filled with satisfaction.

"I'm here."

"That's where you belong."

Her heart thudded in her breast. Oh, if only— She stopped her thoughts. She wasn't willing yet to let in daylight or reason or fear. She stroked his head, sensuously running the curls through her fingers, listening to his steady, strong heartbeat.

"Hold me, Thane," she whispered, and felt his arms tighten. She nestled her head against his shoulder and her hair spread out over both of them.

A long, shuddering sigh escaped him. His fingers trailed lightly up and down her body, caressing, stroking in a manner that was soothing and reassuring. Gradually, she relaxed. She relaxed so much she dozed. When she awoke she was disoriented, then she stirred and remembered and finally faced reality.

She shifted away from Thane and knew how Eve felt after giving Adam the fruit. Why had she done that? She sat up and pulled the sheet about her, gazing around the room that was so typical of him. A wooden toy car sat on the floor along with nuts and bolts and a tool kit. Various tools were scattered about the room, and a hammer, some wires and bolts lay in a pile on the floor beside the bed. A black Stetson hung on one of the posts of the bed. Two pairs of boots stood in the corner along with Bzzip. The room proclaimed "male" clearly. And what a male! Concerned about his son, big, and virile, Thane was sensitive, sexy, too dammed attractive. Only a foot away on a chair, was his open suitcase.

A photograph peeked out from under a knit shirt. She leaned over and picked it up. It was a picture of a smiling woman with dark eyes and red hair. She replaced it carefully and glanced around to find Thane watching her intently.

"Honey . . ."

"Not now, Thane. Please."

He studied her, but lay still. She rose, blushing beneath his gaze, and retrieved her gown, dropping it swiftly over her head.

"Laurel, come here. It won't hurt if you lie in my arms."

My, was that a whopper! She looked at him steadily. "I'd better go to my room."

"Don't be ridiculous, honey. Come here."

She shook her head and reached for the light, flicking the switch twice before she remember the blown fuse. She heard a rustle and felt a rising sense of panic as she saw him sit up, then stand.

She pitched him his jeans and he caught them easily, saying, "I'll get the fuse." But when he'd stepped into the jeans and fastened them, he walked over to her and wrapped his arms around her.

"Thane, give me time to think."

"What's the matter with your breathing?"

"It'll return to normal."

"Why don't we go downstairs and have a cup of coffee?"

That should be safe enough. She wondered how many ways she would try to fool herself. "Fine."

They descended the steps and she fixed the coffee while he found the blown fuse and threw the switches. And while she worked, she examined what had happened, how much difference their loving had made. Just about as much as if the Grand Canyon had moved to her backyard. If she had been aware of Thane before, her consciousness of him now was twice as intense. Everything between them had been heightened, had become more significant, more difficult to cope with. She had stepped out of her shell into his arms and the shock was still reverberating throughout her system. But now she wanted to retreat into her shell, even if she carried with her the memories of this night and the knowledge that he would wait for her to come out again. Thane had his patient moments. And they bound her to him as strongly as the wild times. He passed through the kitchen and went upstairs to see if he had thrown the right switch. She could have saved him the trip. He hit all the right switches.

When he returned, they sat down at the kitchen table. He stretched his long legs beside hers, barely touching her, but nevertheless singeing her flesh. Oh my, she had definitely let herself in for a much bigger struggle. Her body didn't have the foggiest idea about the wariness in her brain. To the finest hair's-breadth setting, her body was attuned to his. She drank the hot coffee, smiled into his blue eyes, and couldn't keep her mind on a word that was said for the first ten minutes.

Finally, she shifted away, out of his reach. The corners of his mouth curled in a satisfied, patient smile, an "I-can-wait-because-I'm-winning" smile.

He refilled their cups, stroking her shoulders as

he passed her. The simple caress sent her mind searching desperately for some safe topic of conversation. She remembered their interrupted discussion about Ronnie, and when he sat down, she plunged into the matter determinedly.

"Thane, have you ever considered a private school?"

"No." Hitching his chair closer, he trailed his fingers lightly along her cheek and it took all her will power to keep her mind on their conversation.

"I called some private schools today and their classes are small. Very small. The children get individual attention."

His brows furrowed as he frowned. "Look, I know what my son needs." He straightened, moving away from her while he picked up his cup and looked at her over it. She caught the note of agony in his voice. "You've seen how shy Ronnie is. For a while he wouldn't play, he wouldn't eat. He became so thin." Thane's voice deepened. "I'm trying to make up for before, for losing his mother, for not having me. . . ."

His eyes were full of torment. In a swift, angry movement he rose and carried his cup to the sink, pouring out the coffee and rinsing the cup. Keeping his back to her, he went on. "Pam and I married in college at Ohio University. I was there on a scholarship. When I graduated, I went to work for an older man who, after the first year, took me in as a partner. In two years I bought him out and he retired. The business grew, I invested in other things. After Ronnie was born, I traveled a lot. Most of the time I wasn't home with him. Business was demanding, I was more interested . . ."

He sounded choked. She felt as if her heart would break in two. He turned to her, looking torn with pain, his eyes bleak, a muscle working in his jaw.

She rose, crossing the room to him, and lightly touched his arm. "Thane, it might not have been as bad as you think. Children adjust—"

"I should've spent more time with him, with Pam. I won't do that again. I won't send him off with a bunch of strangers to school all day."

She couldn't resist. He looked too hurt. She put her arms around him, holding him tightly as she rested her cheek against his chest. Soft curls matted beneath her flesh, tickling her skin. She heard the deep, regular thump of his heart. "You might be overreacting. And it could be as harmful to Ronnie as the other was."

He put his arms around her and held her, his cheek against the top of her head. When he finally spoke, his voice was hoarse. She felt a shudder run through his large body. "He's so damn little. He looks at me with his big eyes and I hate myself for ever being away from him. . . ."

"Thane, don't do that to yourself!" She raised her head to look at him.

"I can't send him to school. I can't send him away from me."

"For his sake, you ought to try. What'll happen if you can't market your toys? If you have to go back to construction work? He'll have to go to school then and it may be much harder on him."

"I'll market the toys."

The words were quiet and as unyielding as iron. She felt drained of strength.

They stood quietly holding each other and she wondered if she had made him hurt more. Her gaze drifted to the window.

"It'll be dawn soon. We should probably get some

sleep before the boys arrive, demanding their breakfast."

"Good idea. Let's go to bed, Laurel."

Her heart failed. Just stopped completely, then started like a jerky, old car engine, sputtering and revving in a ridiculous manner.

"Look here . . ." She met his smile.

"Just wanted to see what reaction I'd get," he said cheerily.

"Let me adjust," she whispered in a sincere plea.

His smile vanished instantly as he studied her. "Sometimes, honey, you just think too much." He leaned down to kiss her, to start the wild, swift hunger that always flared at his touch. She locked her arms around him, returning his kiss while his hands drifted down her back.

With a quick movement, she suddenly stepped out of his embrace and held her hand against his chest. "Thane, don't, please. Not now. Give me room and time."

His blue eyes narrowed, then he said softly, "You'd better go quickly."

She did, almost breaking into a run when she was out of the kitchen. She closed the door to her room, leaning against it breathlessly. How long she stood in one spot, she didn't know, but the sky had lightened to gray as a calm, quiet hush settled on the house. Exhaustion filled her, coming as silently as the pearly dawn. She stretched out on the bed, smiling, tossing aside her worries with a carelessness that would have made Thane grin if he had known. She rubbed her cheek against the pillow, lost in memories of the night, then see-sawed back into the world again, then relished what had happened between them. Gray faded to pink, to glorious rays that splashed through the window panes, falling over the bed and catching the midnight glints in her hair as she settled back and drifted to sleep.

When she finally opened her eyes and glanced at the clock, she saw it was just after nine and that she had slept later than usual. She flung aside the covers, bathed and dressed in jeans and a white shirt. When she entered the sunny kitchen, she found a note in a large, scrawling hand. Thane was working on his house.

After drinking a glass of orange juice, she walked around the block to his house. The sound of hammering echoed in the crisp Saturday morning air. Pausing beneath the cool shade of a tall pine in Thane's front yard, she gazed with wonder at the sight of her brother working with a hammer, tearing loose the burned boards in the front porch. A ladder was against the side of the house and Thane stood on it, prying loose a burned timber in the roof. As she gazed at him, her emotions changed from surprise to a primitive reaction. He was stripped to the waist, his tight jeans clinging low on his hips. His skin was damp, the coppery muscles glistening in the sunlight. He turned his head, saw her, and flashed white teeth as he grinned.

"Hi. Want to work?"

"No, thanks. I'll leave it to you two. Where's Ronnie?"

About that time the small boy appeared around the corner of the house, carrying an empty bucket to Horace. He smiled. "Hi, Mrs. Fortier."

"Have you had breakfast?"

Ronnie nodded. "Dad fixed us breakfast. He said you were asleep, to be quiet, and not wake you."

"Brett, I mean, Laurel, the tent's super! Greg's coming back tonight. And you ought to see the neat tree house Mr. Prescott has."

"I can just imagine." Thane's mocking blue eyes met hers and she suddenly felt a need to get away. "I'll bring sandwiches for lunch."

Thane winked and smiled, fanning the fires that started at the mere sight of his marvelous, fit body.

She went home and puttered aimlessly, doing her laundry, fixing sandwiches and a pitcher of lemonade. How could she get through another evening with him? Steadily, persistently, he was doing just what he had predicted, unwrapping the protective layers around her heart, and she knew it was only a matter of time until . . . Until what? Until she was hopelessly in love with him? Or, until he was finished with the affair, leaving her with another broken heart to mend, to pick up the pieces of her life again? Never! Her hands balled into fists. It was better to go through life without feeling any emotion than to see-saw between heaven and hell.

She paced the kitchen, running her hand over her head. How could she avoid another intimate evening with him? Thane's tent would lure the boys away again.

He hadn't been back in Shreveport very long. Maybe if he met someone else, he would lose interest. For an instant the thought of him with another woman shocked her. Was that really what she wanted? Yet, tonight, if they stayed alone, she knew what the outcome would be. Instead she could have an informal dinner party and invite a woman for Thane and a man for herself. She clamped her jaw closed and tried to think of who to invite.

The vision of Marie Anderson came to mind. The secretary at the office would be perfect. Golden-haired, green-eyed Marie was beautiful, sexy, and intelligent. Laurel liked her and over coffee occasionally listened to Marie's confidences about her private life. Between men at the moment, Marie would be perfect. Now, what male could she invite? There were so few in her life. She thought of Charles Wicks. Older than Jordan by eight years, he was a close friend of her brother's. He was a snob and dull, but safe.

Gritting her teeth she sat down at the phone and called Marie first. Marie was delighted to accept, overwhelmed by Laurel's description of Thane. When Laurel lowered the receiver she stared at it. Something hurt inside, hurt badly. She didn't want to watch Thane turn his charm on Marie, yet the pain made her realize just how far gone she was already. Gone clear to hell and back. Or rather, to heaven and back.

Inexplicably angry with her own dinner plans, yet determined, she called Charles. He politely agreed to come around half-past seven. Laurel hurried to the grocery store, then lunched with Thane and the boys, and didn't find an opportunity or the courage to mention her dinner plans to Thane. When they went back to work on the house, she returned home to fry chicken. With each minute regrets over the dinner arrangements grew, but she was determined to see it through, to keep people and distance between Thane and herself.

Late in the afternoon she heard a clatter outside. The moment Thane appeared he brought magic, like a carnival coming to life, full of bright promises, excitement, joy. Beneath the wild, crazy vitality was a warm, tender heart. Oh, Thane!

She turned to face him as he came through the back door with all the quiet of a hurricane.

Eight

His boots thumped with each step. The door banged closed behind him as he dropped tools in a pile on the floor and straightened. She felt over-powered. His broad chest was bare and shiny with perspiration. His jeans rode low on his narrow hips, the denim clinging to his hard, muscular legs like a second skin. He was dusty, sweaty, totally masculine, and so appealing it took her breath away and sent her heartbeat soaring.

"Hi, gorgeous."

His husky voice started a shiver slithering down her spine. She hoped she sounded normal. "Hi. Want something cold to drink?"

"A beer sounds good." He got a can out of the refrigerator. "I thought I'd take the boys out for some hamburgers, then you and I can go out to dinner."

"Thank you, but . . ." She paused and took a deep breath, suddenly wishing she had done something else besides invite Marie and Charles. "I've invited guests and we'll have an informal dinner, a buffet. We can eat on the patio."

He set the beer down on the counter and turned to her. His eyes, as clear as a Louisiana summer sky, seemed to envelop her. It was difficult to keep her gaze from continually wandering over the inviting mat of curls on his chest. "Guests?" His baritone voice revealed a twinge of annoyance. "I wanted to spend the evening with you."

"Well, I thought it was best this way." Her nerves fluttered. Dangerously. She had to curb a ridiculous urge to wring her hands.

His eyes narrowed. "Who's coming?"

"Marie Anderson, our secretary, and Charles Wicks. Charles is a friend of Jordan's."

"Do Charles and Marie date?" Thane hooked his thumbs into his jeans' pockets, making them slide an inch lower. A tantalizing strip of pale flesh was revealed below his navel and the thin line of hair that ran down from his chest out of sight below the faded jeans. Her gaze drifted lower, over the tight denim. "You didn't answer my question," he said dryly. "Your attention is somewhere else."

Startled, she realized her thoughts had been on his lean hips and long legs. She lifted her gaze and asked, "What did you say?"

His eyes were throwing sparks at her, making her long for a shield.

"Do Charles and Marie date?" he repeated.

Her uneasiness increased by bounds and she raised her chin. "They know each other."

"Answer my question."

She clamped her lips closed a moment, then said, "No, they don't. I've gone out with Charles—"

"Son-of-a-gun! He's one of those sexless wonders you've dated, one of those safe, dull men—"

"Now, look here. Charles is an old friend."

"Uh-huh. And what about Marie? Why is Marie coming? To keep Charles company?"

She felt a blush start along her throat and creep into her cheeks. "I thought it might be nice for you two to get to know each other."

The silence extended for so long that she began to grow nervous again. Tension strained until she snapped. "Well?"

"Well." He crossed the room and tilted her face up with one callused finger. "You coward."

"Maybe so, but it's done now. I told Marie about all your virtues. She's a super person. You should like her."

"I wanted to spend the evening with you. Period. And you knew that."

"Don't complain until you've met her."

"Call them back and tell them I came down with the mumps."

"I can't. Give Marie a chance."

"Why don't you give me a chance?"

"A chance? Ho, you've had more than a chance! You move in like a Sherman tank, a cyclone—cutting a swath that's incredible!" He leaned his arm up against the top of the refrigerator, blocking her once again into a corner between the refrigerator, the counter, and his body. "Do I now? Incredible?"

She began to feel desperate. His large body blanked out the world. She gazed at the strong cords in his throat, in his arms. She tried to avoid looking at his chest with its curling mat of hair that was so soft, so tantalizing. "There are other women in the world," she said, cursing the huskiness in her voice. "Women who are more . . ."

"More what?" He leaned closer. His blue eyes held her in his spell.

For a moment she couldn't answer, then finally snapped, "Just more womanly!"

"Impossible. If I weren't dirty and sweaty from

work, I'd take you in my arms right now and kiss that nonsense away."

White heat speared through her limbs. She couldn't breathe.

"And you want me too," he added arrogantly.

She lifted her chin. "No!"

"No, huh? Your face is raised, your lips are parted . . . some no!"

She blinked, realizing he was right. Anger began to return. "Let me out of this corner, Thane Prescott! You box me in too often!"

His voice dropped to the sensuous note that came when he was passionate. "Okay, Laurel. Dinner for four. I'll get my revenge. Want to take a bet on how long our guests stay?"

"They'll stay. You may thank me for the rest of your life. Marie is beautiful, intelligent, fun—"

He cupped her face in one warm hand and her heart needed intensive care. "Sorry, babe. I'm not interested. I'm overcome and all I can see is long, long black hair, big gray eyes, gorgeous legs, a tiny waist. . . ."

Each word was a stroke, a caress that made breathing difficult, that wiped out her thoughts. She struggled to break free from his spell, from the wizardry of his deep blue eyes. "It won't be long until they get here." Her voice was breathy, soft. "I'll run to McDonald's and get burgers for the boys."

"I'll go. What time will company arrive?"

"I don't know." She couldn't think about anything but his firm, teasing lips, his blue eyes, his male body.

He raised an eyebrow. "That's more like it!"

She realized something had happened that shouldn't have. She shook her head. "What did you ask me? See what I mean about a cyclone!"

He chuckled. "I believe you just told me that you don't know what time your guests will arrive."

"They'll be here at seven-thirty!"

"What a waste of time." His gaze drifted lazily over her, setting her on fire.

"I'd better get ready," she murmured, not moving. "Will you let me out of the corner?"

"As I said, if I weren't so dirty from work . . ."

Her heart thudded. If only he knew that at that moment she didn't care. Desire was dancing in her like dust devils on a windy prairie. She wouldn't resist if his arms closed around her. She wanted them to. She wanted to pull his hard, dusty body close, to feel his strong arms envelop her, to have his mouth take hers. She stared at him blankly as he said, "I'll feed the hungry wolves. Where are your car keys?"

And she did it again. She knew he had asked her something, but what the hell was it? Seconds ticked past. He smiled. "Score one more for me," he said softly. "Keys, honey. Where are the car keys?"

She wanted to fling them at him. She picked them up off the counter and held them out. With a mocking smile, he took the keys to her Honda, ran upstairs for a shirt, and hurried out the door, leaving her aching with longing for him. How could he breeze in and turn everything upside down so swiftly? He would be bored stiff with Charles, but maybe Marie would make up for the dull moments. Laurel gritted her teeth at the thought, then went upstairs to bathe and wash her hair, aware that she was listening for any sound of Thane in the house.

Back in her bedroom she surveyed the dresses hanging neatly in her closet. Something dull, plain . . . She selected a simple pale blue cotton shirtwaist and navy high-heeled sandals. Carefully, she braided her hair into one long plait, then wound it around her head and fastened it securely. Extra securely.

She was dressed and ready to go downstairs when she heared the kitchen door bang shut. She met him at the head of the stairs. His gaze took in her outfit with a slow appraisal that started all the motors again.

"Wow."

"It can't be," she said dryly, thinking she should be the one to say wow. He looked so damn virile and male, even with dust on his cheeks and throat and arms, his hands dirty from work. He looked earthy, with vitality radiating from him.

He paused about a foot from her and raised an eyebrow, his hands on his hips. "Trying to be Little Miss Prim tonight?"

"Could be."

In a sardonic drawl, he said, "Well, for your information," he drawled, "the shape under that cotton dress is far from prim."

"You're going to be late!"

"Getting scared?"

"No." She couldn't resist flinging back the gauntlet.

Sparks clashed between them and he moved closer. "My saucy wench, you look as prim as Salome. That neat little blue dress just makes me want to take you in my arms and crush—"

Aflame from his words, the hungry look in his eyes, she tried to stop him. "They'll be here in twenty minutes."

"Want to make a wager with me?"

Suspicious, yet too curious to resist, she asked, "What kind of wager?"

His voice dropped, a husky note starting ripples

in her. "Before this night is out, I'll have that long raven hair of yours unbraided."

The warmth uncoiling inside her burst into flame. She tried to hide it beneath a firm voice. "I won't wager anything with you. I have to get dinner."

"Want some help?"

"No, thank you. I have everything under control."

"Everything, Laurel?"

His tone, the innuendo, started another cascade of sparks showering down her spine. "Yes. I'll leave all your time free to get to know Marie."

"Maybe. Maybe I have other plans for the evening."

"Marie and Charles are definitely not the same type, so don't get ideas there."

"My ideas are taken completely by one person, one fascinating, intriguing, beautiful woman."

The message in his eyes matched his words, making her tremble. It was an effort to go and her voice sounded breathless as she said, "I'll be downstairs." She rushed down the steps, his words swirling in her mind. "Fascinating, beautiful . . ." Why did Thane have to be so charming, so able to leap over her defenses as if they didn't exist? Too charming and too wild! At the foot of the steps she looked up. His thick dark curls framing his head, he stood at the rail, watching her. Her heart thudded violently. Defenses didn't exist against him. His blue eyes melted them, pierced them like a laser. With her breathing unsteady, she went to the kitchen and began working furiously to get everything ready.

Marie arrived first and when Laurel saw her, her expectations swung between high and low.

Her golden hair falling softly over her shoulders,

her make-up flawless, her pale yellow dress fitting to perfection, Marie Anderson was ravishing. How could he look at anyone else?

"Hi, Brett."

"Come in. You look great!"

"Thanks." Marie lowered her voice. "I can't wait to meet this gorgeous hunk you told me about."

"He'll be down in a minute."

"He stays here?"

"Lower your eyebrows, Marie. His home burned. He's staying here temporarily with me, Horace, Dad, his son . . ."

Marie laughed. "My eyebrows are lowered."

"Here comes Charles."

Marie looked over her shoulder. "Oh, yes, Charles. Mr. Wicks. He won't be happy to see a little secretary here, rubbing elbows on the same level with him."

"Don't pay any attention. He's not the one you need to notice."

"Don't worry. I'm waiting for Mr. Thane Prescott!"

Laurel watched Charles Wicks cross the walk and felt a leaden weight settle in the pit of her stomach. She had given up an evening alone with Thane for Charles Wicks. Charles was tall, stoop-shouldered, immaculately dressed in a silk shirt and gray slacks. With his pale brown eyes and narrow chin he would fade into oblivion when Thane entered the room. "Evening Brett, Marie."

"If you two will come in," Laurel said. They moved into the living room and Marie and Charles sat down while Laurel mixed drinks. She handed them their drinks, then sat in a brown wingback chair facing Charles, who sat on the sofa, and Marie, who sat in another chair.

Charles lifted his drink. "Talked to Jordan

today. He's investing in Zolta Mining. Tried to tell me how good it is. Said your father thinks so too. Where is the judge?"

"Dad's at Caddo Lake on a fishing trip." Laurel glanced at her watch. Where was Thane?

"When will he be back?"

"He'll be here Wed—"

"Laurel!" Thane's deep voice from upstairs interrupted her.

Startled, she smiled hesitantly at her guests. "Just a minute, excuse me."

"He calls you Laurel?" Marie asked.

"My first name. Laurel Brett."

"Quaint," Charles murmured.

She rose to her feet, but before she'd taken a step, Thane called again, "Darlin', have you seen my tiger-striped briefs?"

Laurel stiffened. Raging flames burned up through the soles of her feet, a blush consuming her as if she had been set on fire. Thane had just delivered life's most embarrassing moment to her, wrapped in gold and all tied up with red ribbons! How could she face Charles and Marie for the next few hours? Or even the next few minutes? She felt like shaking her fist at the empty doorway. Mr. T. Prescott—"T" for trouble!

Marie raised her brows and smiled. "Sure you meant to invite me to meet him?"

"I'm sure," Laurel gritted through clenched teeth. Charles had turned as red as she felt and was staring at her intently.

Trying to gather the tatters of her dignity, she raised her chin. "Excuse me a minute."

The walk out of the room was endless misery. The minute she rounded the corner she rushed toward the stairs. At the top she collided with him.

His hands reached out to steady her. "Whoa. You

didn't have to run right up here. I found some others."

"Damn you!" She struggled to keep her voice low. "Of all the cheap, rotten tricks you've pulled, this is the worst!"

"Cheap, rotten tricks?" he asked innocently.

"I see that damned dimple and the laughter in your eyes! So help me . . . Charles Wicks doesn't have any sense of humor. He's worse than Lamont or Jordan, if anyone could be."

"Then why is he sitting in your living room at your invitation?"

"Don't start quizzing me like I'm the one who needs my head examined!"

"I'll be happy to examine your head, or any other part—"

"Will you be serious! Do you know what you've done with that question about your underwear? You probably do," she answered her question, feeling swamped, as if she were combating an impossible force. "That was deliberate."

"It sure was. Maybe you'll learn a lesson about interfering when I plan a marvelous evening with my special girl."

My special girl. The words wound through her, warming her, melting her anger, making her want to send Marie and Charles home. Special. His eyes twinkled, his dimple was adorable, his smile devastating. He was dressed in a navy blue cotton shirt that was open at the throat to reveal the dark inviting curls on his chest and that accentuated his bronze skin and deep blue eyes. It was tucked into dark slacks that fit his trim hips snugly. How could she resist him? Her anger evaporated.

He tilted her chin up. "Do I see a smile about to surface?"

"You might. You've charmed your way through another crisis."

"Have I really?"

"You know you could. Are you going to embarrass me again?"

"Wait and see. Maybe they'll go home early if I keep it up."

"That's what you want, isn't it?"

"Sure." He dropped his arm around her shoulders. She shrugged it away.

"Look, Charles sees Jordan and Lamont all the time. I come from a stiff-necked, old-fashioned family. Don't complicate my life unnecessarily."

"I wouldn't dream of it," he answered blandly and she felt as if she were standing in the center of a mine field.

"Promise me you'll keep your hands to yourself when we get downstairs."

"I'll try."

"Try isn't good enough."

"It'll have to do." Mischief danced in his eyes.

"I'm not sure I can face them again."

"Want me to go down and tell them to go away?"

"No, dammit!"

"My, you're getting worked up."

She stared at him as his grin widened. "Don't say another word, Thane Prescott! Our guests are waiting."

"I just remembered something. You go ahead."

She didn't want to face Marie and Charles alone, but she descended the stairs and entered the living room. Charles looked at her curiously for a moment before glancing away. Trying to assume an air of dignity in spite of the blush burning her cheeks, Laurel said, "Mr. Prescott will be right down."

There was an uncomfortable silence. While

Charles stared out the window, Marie looked faintly amused.

Footsteps sounded in the hall, a clatter of boots on the polished oak. "Darlin'!" Like a whirlwind Thane charged into the room, crossing the living room without hesitation to sweep Laurel into his arms, bending over her for a kiss.

He smelled like a brewery! What had he done since she left him, for God's sake? Bathed in bourbon? Her eyes flew wide open in shock. He bent her over further until she felt as if she would fall. She automatically clung to his shoulders, her protest dying in her throat as he kissed it away. Kissed it away completely. Laurel thought he would never stop. She couldn't beat against his chest in front of Marie and Charles. She was helpless as he explored her mouth thoroughly. It was a burning, passionate kiss that went on and on until she forgot her embarrassment, forgot Marie and Charles. Suddenly, Thane swung her upright, releasing her.

She almost fell on her face. She swayed and his arm reached out. "Steady, darlin'."

Fury consumed her and along with it, embarrassment streaked through her like a brush-fire. When she turned her head to look at him, Thane pursed his lips and stepped away.

Before she could speak, he slipped his arm around her and tucked her against him, all the while smiling at Marie who was holding back laughter.

"Sorry," he said blithely. "I just get carried away. Two whole minutes have passed since I last saw my li'l darlin'."

Laurel felt an uncontrollable urge to shake her fist at him again. The alcoholic fumes were threatening to overcome her and she just stopped herself from fanning the air. When she tried to twist free, his arms tightened, holding her pasted to his side. There wasn't anything else to do except make introductions.

"Marie, I want you to meet Thane Prescott." Her breathy voice trembled. She tried to get it under control. "Thane, this is Marie Anderson and this is Charles Wicks."

Charles's face was scarlet as he rose to his feet. He looked as if he had bitten into something sour as his eyes darted back and forth between Laurel and Thane while he shook hands stiffly and coughed.

Struggling again to wriggle free, Laurel wondered if she would spend the evening like Thane's Siamese twin, joined at the hips. "Can I get you a drink?" she asked him with deadly sweetness.

He looked down, his blue eyes dancing with devilment. "You better believe you can, li'l darlin'. Just the usual, bourbon and branch water."

His arm dropped away from her waist and he sat down to talk to Marie and Charles. The usual. Laurel glanced at him. He was determined to drive Marie and Charles away as speedily as possible.

Charles settled back in his seat and crossed his legs. Swinging his foot nervously, he asked, "Do you live in Shreveport?"

"Right here in this house, at least until the good judge returns," Thane answered with maddening cheer. He smiled at Laurel. "Or until li'l darlin' sends me away."

She glared at him, mixing his drink as fast as possible, the ice cubes clinking and clattering while she stirred violently. Jordan and Lamont would develop apoplexy when Charles relayed this conversation.

Charles's foot swung faster and Marie raised a quizzical eyebrow at Laurel.

Charles tried again. "Where do you work?"

"I don't. I'm relying on li'l darlin' to get me going."

Charles choked on his drink, eyeing Laurel intently.

"What he means," she said furiously, "is that he's waiting on me to patent his toys. He's an inventor. He invents all sorts of things." She gave Thane as dark a look as possible.

He smiled blandly when she approached with his drink. Laurel stepped on his toe. His smile widened, the dimple deepening. When she held the drink out to him, his fingers closed around her waist.

She tried to tip the drink and dump it in his lap, but his fingers tightened like an iron clamp and she couldn't move her wrist. He took the drink and set it on a table beside his chair.

"Come here, li'l darlin', sit on my lap."

She shook her head violently and in a syrupy sweet voice asked, "May I see you a moment in the kitchen?"

"Sure thing." He winked broadly at Marie. "She just can't keep her hands off me."

As soon as they were in the kitchen she shook her fist at him. "Dammit, Thane!"

"Oh, ho. Little aggravated?"

"Don't you 'li'l darlin' ' me one more time! Marie is convulsed with laughter and Charles is in shock."

"My goodness, that's too bad. Ready to ask them to leave?"

"No! You may be back in the tent with the boys tonight!" His twinkling blue eyes sent showers raining on her fiery anger, spattering out the blaze. "I've never lost control like I have with you. I wanted to throw that drink at you. What did you do? Shower in Old Crow?"

"Dabbed a little here and there. It'll fade fast."

"After they've decided your bloodstream is ninety-nine percent alcohol! And what's the matter with you anyway? Marie is gorgeous."

"Which one is Marie?"

"Your charm isn't going to get you out of this one. When dinner is over, comes the hour of retribution."

"Sounds intriguing. I'd love to retribute with you."

She felt her anger slipping, teetering on the brink of oblivion. His voice changed suddenly, the teasing vanished. He moved closer, close enough so that she caught the now faint scent of bourbon, tinged with an inviting, male scent. "When you're angry," he said softly, "your gray eyes darken, your cheeks turn pink, and your voice gets that deep, breathless quality. Did you know you react the same way during your most passionate moments?"

Anger dropped over the edge and was gone. She couldn't stop her reaction to his seductive words. She licked dry lips, felt her heart thud. "No matter how heinous your crimes, you can charm your way out of trouble."

"I hope so. Honey, let's get rid of the company."

She was melting and wanted to wind her arms around his strong shoulders and let him crush her against his chest. She couldn't and it hurt.

"We can't. I invited them for dinner and it's almost ready."

"We can pack doggie bags."

"Not on your life!" A smile threatened and she clamped her lips shut.

"Wonder what's going through their thoughts right now."

"Oh my word! You get back out there. And don't smirk and leer when you do."

"Me? Smirk and leer?" he asked, so innocently that she smiled. She trailed her finger along his jaw. "Cyclone Prescott. You did it again."

"Did what?"

"Turned my world upside-down. Devastated everything in your path. Will you please go?"

"You tell me I've devastated you, look at me with your smoky eyes, and then ask me to go?"

She stepped back. "Go. Please, go."

His gaze drifted slowly down to her feet, then returned to meet hers, leaving a fiery trail in its wake. "You're a responsive woman, hiding from life. You react to a glance." His gaze dropped to her breasts, the thrusting peaks taut beneath the thin cotton dress. "Laurel, before this night is out, you'll let your hair down. You'll let it down for me or I'll take it down," he promised in a husky, determined voice that made her tremble.

"Thane . . ."

"I'm going."

She watched his broad back, the mass of thick soft curls on the back of his head, his narrow hips, as he went through the door and she had to fight a ridiculous surge of excitement. Her emotion changed when she remembered the whole purpose of the evening. With a sigh, she smoothed her skirt and thought about Marie, wondering if she had made a mistake. She had begun to loosen, to vacillate between throwing up defenses and letting them down. She had to have time to think. Time and room. Marie could give her a little if she held Thane's attention even for a little while.

Grimly, she entered the living room. "Charles,"

she said, "would you come into the kitchen a moment? I want to ask you about something."

Looking acutely uncomfortable, as if he was afraid she might throw herself at him, Charles said, "Of course."

Thane frowned. "Charley, the last man who laid a hand on my li'l darlin' spent four days in traction."

Charles paled and blinked. Laurel crossed the room to take his arm. "Don't pay any attention to him, Charles. He's joking." She led him out of the room.

In the kitchen she picked up the morning paper to ask Charles the only question she knew would keep him talking at length while Marie and Thane were alone together. "Can you tell me the best stock for a long-term investment, something with a low yield?"

Charles glanced nervously toward the closed kitchen door. "Perhaps we should take the paper into the front room, Brett."

"Oh, no. You know it's of no interest to Marie or Thane."

"Have you known him long?"

"No, Charles. There's nothing between us."

He laughed uneasily. "No, of course not. Does Jordan know this Prescott?"

"Yes, Jordan met him Thursday evening." Thursday evening seemed a thousand years ago. Charles launched into a dry recital of possible investments, but Laurel's mind was on the time, on Thane and Marie.

The timer pinged, interrupting the stock market discussion. Potatoes, cooked in the half-shell and topped with golden cheese, were done. Marie stepped into the kitchen, a smile on her face. "May I help? I heard a timer."

"I'll leave you ladies," Charles said and fled to the living room.

Marie leaned against the counter. "Bre—Laurel."

"Brett's fine."

"I think you're going to be called Laurel for a long, long time. There's only one woman Thane Prescott is interested in. Are you sure about what you want?"

"Very. Marie, don't give up. I'll take care of dinner. Go back in there and dazzle him."

"Those sexy blue eyes can see only you. He told me he's been teasing you with that 'li'l darlin'' business."

Laurel sighed. "Slightly. He has a warped sense of humor."

"He's adorable. I don't know how you resist."

"I'll get dinner. Go enjoy the men."

With a shrug Marie smiled and left. Laurel placed the oven-fried chicken on a large platter but her thoughts weren't on the chicken. She *didn't* resist Thane. She hadn't last night. Should she at all? Shoving aside her worries, she set a covered basket of hot rolls beside the golden chicken. When she was ready, she summoned the others.

Everyone served themselves from the dishes spread along the kitchen counter, then they ate out on the cool patio, enjoying the crisp air of the fall evening. Afterward, Marie helped Laurel stack dishes in the kitchen. Once Laurel glanced out at the lighted patio to see Charles listening intently to something Thane was telling him. He's charmed Charles too, she thought, feeling hopelessly lost in a morass of contradictory emotions. She shooed Marie outside to join the men and in a few minutes had the kitchen cleaned.

Barely half an hour after dinner, Marie rose and said she had to get home. Charles stood also.

"Time for me to go along, too," he said. "It's been"—there was the barest pause before he finished—"an interesting evening, Brett." He offered his hand to Thane. "Good to meet you, Prescott. I'll look into that drilling company. Glad to hear about it."

As she walked to the door with Marie, Laurel said, "Are you sure you can't stay longer? I'll disappear upstairs."

They reached the door with the men still far behind them down the hall. Marie laughed. "Brett, he doesn't know I exist."

"I don't think so."

"I don't know why you're fighting it. I wouldn't. Not for a second!"

She couldn't answer, so she smiled. "I'm sorry the evening was a waste of time."

"I had fun. It was worth it to see Charles in shock. If you ever find a spare Thane Prescott, give me a call. This one's definitely taken."

The men reached them, they all said good night, and Laurel stood under the porch light watching Marie and Charles leave. But most of her attention was on Thane. She dreaded facing him. They were alone and it was so early in the evening. Only ten o'clock. The minutes stretched as Marie climbed into her Ford and drove away. Charles's Lincoln pulled away from the curb and disappeared down the street.

There wasn't anything else to do. Laurel turned around.

Nine

Thane was lounging in the doorway, his broad shoulder against the jamb, one hand in his pants pocket, one dark brow raised as he watched her. His smoldering gaze made her heart drum and her nerves flutter.

"Well, you succeeded," she said. "You drove them away and it's only ten."

"And now there's just you and me." His husky voice set off sparks. She couldn't catch her breath. He straightened and stepped back. "Come in, Laurel."

Her knees felt weak. He was so handsome, so virile. When she walked through the door, they would be alone and his seductive, hooded blue eyes conveyed clearly what he had in mind.

"Why do I so often get the feeling that I'm a guest in my own home? Everywhere you go, you take over."

He took her arm and drew her inside. His rough baritone sent fiery streams coursing in her veins as he said, "There's only one place I want to take over—your heart."

144

Mesmerized by those blue eyes, she stepped inside. He closed the door, locked it, and switched off the lights.

The darkness stirred her out of the spell woven by his voice, his touch, his eyes and words. She steeled herself for an onslaught of his seductive charm. He stood between her and the stairs, effectively blocking her path. "I want to go, Thane. Don't start something. You're going too fast."

"As you said, it's early. Let's have a nightcap."

"Will you get out of my way?"

A slow, lazy smile lifted the corners of his mouth. She felt desperate, her heart raced. His voice was deep, so masculine. "No, Laurel, you're not going to say good night and go," he said softly.

The panicky feeling that he had caused before returned. She backed away a step, bumping into the locked front door. "You've interfered enough! I've told you I don't want your interference."

"The part of you that doesn't is so tiny. All the woman in you does. I'll show you."

He moved a step closer and she began to tremble. How could she combat her body, her physical responses to him that surged to life at his faintest touch?

He reached out and placed both hands on either side of her, leaning his palms against the door, his big body blocking her exit. Even though he wasn't touching her, she gasped, struggling to breathe as she turned her head away. His sinewy, corded arm, tanned and so strong, was inches from her face. She wanted to put her head against his forearm, to forget the pain, but she knew that would make it worse, not better.

"Now, remember what I promised you?"

She didn't want to look into his eyes. She closed hers. "I don't know."

"One promise was, I intend to find out why you hold back, what you're afraid of."

His words tore through her, plunging into her heart sharply. She kept her eyes shut. "Move out of my way and let me go."

"There's no picture of your husband. There's nothing. Was something in your marriage bad?" He asked gently. "Is that why you're so afraid, Laurel?"

Startled, she looked up. Light from the upstairs hall shed enough illumination to see Thane's probing, curious eyes. "Was it bad, honey?"

"Bad? Oh, no!" She felt cornered and was angry that he would push and persist and make her remember. She faced him, her arms stiff at her sides. "No, it wasn't bad. It was heaven. It was perfect. We knew each other such a short time. Our time together, that tiny segment of my life, I think of as golden." And then the memories came rushing up to invade her thoughts, her emotions. She whispered, "Wade had golden hair and when he smiled the world was marvelous. We were so happy, so in love! I adored him and every moment was precious. . . ."

She gasped for breath, her breast heaving as if all oxygen had been cut off. She was furious that he was goading her into revealing so much, into looking back when she didn't want to, into rushing forward too swiftly into another relationship. The empty, hollow feeling that she had fought so hard to overcome was returning with the force of a gale. Somewhere deep inside a terrible cry was trying to surface. Her rage increased as she fought to smother her tears.

Thane frowned, his dark brows drawing together as he studied her. "Then why is your room so bare, why don't—"

"Why don't I have his picture?" she finished for him. "Because everyone has their own way of reacting to loss! My pictures of Wade are here." She placed her fist against her breast, over her heart. "I put it all away. There's no use hanging onto his things, because not one of them will bring him back. . . ."

"Oh, Laurel, shh . . ." His arms wrapped around her, fitting her against his solid, massive chest, holding her to his heart.

He tilted her face up, his eyes searching hers. His thumb raked across her cheek below her eyes. "Laurel, life has to go on. Turn loose of the past." His voice lowered to a whispery baritone that touched her soul. "Let me into your life."

Buffeted by the impact of his blue eyes, she drew a long breath. He leaned forward, his mouth coming down over hers. She struggled against him, pushing at a chest as solid and unyielding as granite. She tried to twist her head away, to close her lips.

His tongue traced her lips, churning the tumult that raged within her. "Stop fighting me," he murmured.

"No!" But when she opened her mouth to protest, she was lost. His arms tightened around her, molding her to his body, as his tongue thrust into her mouth to take ravenous possession, to convey what words couldn't say.

She trembled violently. His eyes flew open momentarily, then his hand slipped down brashly to curve over her buttocks, pulling her hips to his while one arm remained a steel band around her waist. Her hands grew still, resting on his strong arms while her heart raced until it was a thunderous roar in her ears.

His plundering kiss deepened to a fiery, passionate demand that blanked out her fears, her worries about the past or the future. She became conscious only of Thane. She drowned in his kisses, plunging through fathoms into depths beyond her control. A soft moan of pleasure rose in her throat.

His big, hard body felt so good. Her hands slipped up over bulging muscles, over broad shoulders, touching smooth skin and hard bone, to his strong neck. Her fingers wound in his soft curls, relishing their sensual, silky touch.

And still his turbulent kisses continued, driving her beyond one barrier to another and then another.

In a whispery trail that sent shivers down her spine, his rough fingertips stroke the nape of her neck, tracing her ears, her throat, winding up to her head. She felt the pins go, knew he was taking down the long braid of her hair, undoing her hair along with her reluctance.

In his deep voice he murmured, "Laurel, Laurel . . ." Her name rolled off his tongue with a special husky inflection that was branded in her mind forever.

She wanted him so badly, so damn badly, but she was afraid she'd never be enough woman for him, either emotionally or physically. A groan of agony escaped and his eyes narrowed.

"Laurel, honey, what it is?" His blue eyes stripped bare her soul.

"I want you to stop! Leave me in peace."

"What part of you wants me to stop? Your mouth, Laurel?" he whispered as he brushed his lips sensuously over hers, making her throb for him. "Your body?" His big hand traced her curves, her softness, running over hip and thigh, drifting across her stomach. Her hips shifted instinctively. The lightning charges bursting through her made her unaware of his other hand. The heavy braid fell against her back and his fingers began working in it, pulling her hair free.

"You don't want my hands? My mouth?"

"Our kisses can't mean anything to you. I haven't known you that long," she whispered, even as she tilted her head so he could nuzzle her throat, reaching the pulsebeat at the base of her neck.

"You're sweet, you're intelligent . . . I know you're passionate. I look at you and think what a waste. I can't bear the forlorn look in your beautiful gray eyes."

"Stop it, Thane!"

As if he hadn't heard, he continued relentlessly, saying words that touched her as surely as his hands. "That prim dress, so plain, covering a beautiful body . . ." His voice lowered to a husky note that ran riot through her system. "You don't want my hands and mouth here?" His left arm circled her waist and he leaned down, his moist mouth covering the quivering peak of her breast. Through the thin layers of clothing she could feel his heated breath. Devastation. Raw emotions clashed within her as her body responded, her breasts ached with longing for him.

"Don't make love to me!" she gasped. Her head felt heavy, rolling back on her neck. She closed her eyes. How could she push him away? She could only tremble, moan with pleasure, with a primitive, profound need for one man out of all men on earth. Thane. How she needed him, wanted him! She wanted his joy, his exuberance, his liveliness. She yearned for his maleness, his caresses. Swaying toward him, she rested her fingers on his massive shoulders.

He rained kisses over her dress, on her bare flesh

while his fingers tugged at the buttons. He straightened to watch her, his blue eyes blazing into her with passion.

"This dress, your hair, this house—so damn prim. I know better. I won't let you waste away like that." He pushed aside the cotton dress, her slip, her filmy lace bra to cup her breast in his big hand, holding her eager, tremulous flesh, taking her captive. Slowly, with tantalizing deliberation, his thumb grazed the taut peak.

On fire, she gasped. Fabulous pinwheels of sensation whirred in her, fluttering and streaking wildly. His thigh pressed, nudging hers apart, sliding between them; his male hardness bulged against her.

Her heart, her soul cried out for him, for his powerful strength, yet she was afraid. She couldn't bear to lose him, to have an affair, and then get dropped. And what could she give him in return? Emptiness? Since the day she had lost the baby, she had felt inadequate, so incomplete. Dark thoughts rose, steaming up like vapor in a swamp to envelop her. She pushed against him violently.

He pulled back. "What is it, Laurel?"

She felt her throat close with pain. Gasping, she answered, "You're rushing me." Looking down to pull her clothes in place, she saw his slacks, his obvious readiness that made her want to reach for him again.

While she straightened her dress, he watched her unwaveringly until she felt as if he were attempting to hypnotize her. She tried to push away his arms, which were wrapped around her waist.

"Why, honey?" he asked in a voice as soft as rose petals. "What stopped you?"

She didn't want to look into those blue eyes that

could slice through her words and discover her emotions. "You're coming on too fast when I'm uncertain." She couldn't pry her arms free and she couldn't face him. She buttoned her dress. In the heavy silence tension sprang between them, and steeling herself, she finally looked up.

Smoldering blue, like a gale-swept sea, invaded her senses and heightened the upheaval raging within her. "I can't treat love lightly," she said shakily. "It's deeply personal with me and that's just the way I am."

His big, work-roughened fingers, callused from repairing his home, reached out to unfasten a button again.

"Are you listening to me?"

"I heard every word."

"Then what are you doing?" Another button slipped free. His head was bent, his thick, curly lashes lowered. She wanted to place her palm on his tanned cheek, to wind her arms around his neck and pull his mouth down. She didn't.

"Laurel, honey, it won't hurt you to have a little loving."

"No!" The word was explosive. His eyes raised and she braced for another soul-searching stare. "I said we're almost strangers. I know we're not physically, but we are in all other ways. I can't go this fast, Thane."

Seconds ticked past, stretching nerves already strained. "All right, Laurel, we'll get to know each other," he said roughly, and she felt as if an avalanche threatened her. She knew him well enough to know that he went at anything heart and soul. Could she withstand his determination?

He rebuttoned her dress and it was almost as devastating as his unfastening it. She was aware of his knuckles brushing the valley between her breasts, touching the soft curves.

"I'll do that!"

He tilted his head and looked at her with hooded, smoldering eyes. "Your voice is breathless."

"It's getting late." She shook her head and her long, silky hair swirled over her shoulders.

"You want to go to bed?" he asked in husky, seductive tones that almost buckled her knees. She caught her breath.

"You're not helping!"

"You want me to help you go to bed?"

"No, dammit. You know what I mean."

He took a slow, deep breath and a shudder rippled through him. He stretched, reaching out both long arms until his muscles popped and she realized what control he was exercising. "Come on," he said, "we have some getting acquainted to do. You won't be able to sleep anyway, li'l darlin'."

She smiled. "Your conscience should keep you from sleeping."

"It's not my conscience, honey," he drawled, "it's long black hair, gorgeous legs. . . . I want you beside me, in my—"

"Enough! Thank you. Speaking of legs, where's Manuel?"

"In the utility room with a cover over his cage. I tucked him away for the night. I'll be glad to do the same for you."

"You know my answer," she said, and hoped he couldn't hear her heart pounding.

Smiling, he put his arm across her shoulders and led her to the kitchen.

She fixed a glass of tea; Thane settled with a beer. They sat at the table and talked, but all the time his blue eyes blazed at her with unmistakable desire. He stretched out in the chair, one ankle crossed on his knee. While they chatted he stroked her hair, brushing his fingers against her neck, her throat, her shoulder, and each touch played over her sensitive flesh like a violin bow, creating a melody of longing, a duet of desire.

The room became warmer, his voice lower and huskier. Her own became breathless. She knew what was happening between them and she knew it had to stop before they were both burning out of control again. Swiftly, she rose. "I'm going to bed."

"Fine. I will too." He stood, his shoulder brushing hers as he moved away.

The simple act of turning out lights, checking the doors, climbing the stairs together, made the moment intensely intimate. It had a married feeling. Thane dropped his arm across her shoulders as they reached the top of the stairs.

She turned. "Good night."

His arms went around her and his mouth took possession of hers before she could protest. All his touches during the past hour, his lovemaking before that, had her quivering with readiness. Response burst in her and the ballad their hearts played, soared. Eager tongues played an age-old cadenza. Her heart thrummed to a savage beat. She molded herself to his hard body, clinging to him to return his kiss.

They sank to the hard, cold floor and she barely noticed any discomfort. Thane's mouth held her captive while his hands followed her curves, moving with light, deft caresses, unbuttong the dress she had so carefully fastened earlier. He shifted the material off her shoulders, pushing it down as he sat up. His arm circled her waist, lifting her easily to his lap, her attention taken by his hungry lips and tongue. His hands raised her hips to free her of the dress.

She turned her head slightly, her long hair cascading down to hide her eyes from him. His hands moved with certainty as he undressed her. She caught one big hand, holding his warm, rough fingers in hers. "I thought you'd wait, that you understood you're rushing me," she whispered breathlessly.

"Laurel, you don't want to wait now. You're trembling. Trust me, honey." He wound his free hand in her hair and tilted her face up and she was lost in blue. He whispered, "Just trust a little. . . ."

His dark head dipped, lowering to her breast, to kiss the eager up-thrusting peak, to make her gasp and close her eyes and surrender.

Within minutes he had unbuttoned his shirt, flinging it aside. The rest of his clothes followed as he kissed her warm, smooth flesh, his fingers exploring, seeking ways to give her pleasure, stroking her long, lovely legs.

His leg moved between hers, the rough, hard thigh erotic in tactile sensations, then becoming a pressure that made her move and moan in need until she cried out as she reached a peak, then sank and quivered, wanting more.

He shifted his weight, entering her slowly, taking his time in an effort of control that burned away swiftly. The moved together while she clung to his broad back and whispered his name again and again. He took her physically, but it went deeper and she knew it. For one clear second she knew how binding each touch was—a wizard's chain, forged by feather-light caresses, by deep hungry kisses, and linked by sorcery, as binding as steel.

Reason was lost as he carried her over the brink into rapture. Ecstasy burst with blinding radiance, then left her to float gradually down through a quiet night of satisfaction to the hard earth of reality. Twice now he had loved her in the most total sense possible. The loving weighted one part of her life, throwing the rest off balance.

While her stormy thoughts seethed, while she played with his soft hair, he moved her, shifting beneath her, pulling her on top of him. She lay quietly, listening to his heart slow as he stroked her long hair and held her tightly. She couldn't resist him. Did she need to? How did she know what to think in the whirlwind he caused?

"You're rushing me again, Thane," she said softly.

"I lost control."

She didn't believe him for a minute. He continued to stroke her hair and his voice was husky, like warm sunshine falling over her. "You're beautiful, Laurel."

"Give me room. Please. This was wonderful, Thane, better than I could ever imagine, but in every other way we're really strangers."

"I told you, we'll get to know each other." He paused. "In every way."

Why did his statement make her heart jump with eagerness and her fingers clench with caution?

She slipped off him and reached for her clothes. It embarrassed her to sit naked beside him, even while he seemed oblivious to his own nudity.

He sat up and kissed her, softly, oh so lightly, yet his lips made her heart skip a beat. "Come to bed with me, honey," he whispered.

"I can't. Not yet."

His gaze was relentless, searching until he seemed to find some answer. He reached for his slacks and pulled them on. She felt relieved, as if part of her brain could function again. He rose and looked down at her, a half-smile tugging at his mouth. "If this is what you want . . . 'Night, Laurel." He turned and went to his room, closing the door behind him.

She stared at the door. All she had to do was follow him, call to him—and she longed to. She wanted to lie in his arms the rest of the night, but morning always came and with the clear light of reason could also come pain and regret.

Finally, she went to her room for a troubled, dream-filled sleep. The next day, Thane did just what he promised—tried to get to know her. They went to church together, took Ronnie, Horace, and Greg out to eat with them, then left the boys at Thane's and drove to Bossier City to Louisiana Downs. They sat at a table in the upper level, didn't touch a bite of what they'd ordered, and missed all the races while they talked and looked at each other.

Ronnie and Horace came home to sleep because Monday was a school day. They played Thane's game, Victory, for an hour until both boys finally went upstairs to bed.

Sitting cross-legged on the floor in jeans and a gray sweat shirt, Laurel looked at Thane. "Ronnie should be off to school tomorrow, too."

He raised his head to look at her. "I've given it some more thought. I've talked to him about it, too. He doesn't want to go."

"Of course he doesn't want to! He's shy. It's only natural at his age that he'd feel reluctant, but it wouldn't take him any time to adjust. He fit in here without a ripple. He's trailed around with Greg and Horace all weekend and he's been fine."

Thane's blue eyes were dark and brooding while he thought over what she said. His big shoulders heaved as he sighed. "I don't know. I want what's best for him."

"When Tuesday comes, there's really no need for you to go to a motel. You and Ronnie are welcome to stay here."

He smiled. "Thanks, but I'll get out of this house. And someday I'll get—" He stopped abruptly.

She tilted her head to one side. "You'll get what?"

"I'll tell you later." He winked, but she had a feeling she wouldn't ever know what he had started to say.

Monday morning Horace went to school, Laurel to the office, and Thane went home to meet the carpenters who were to work on his house. Tuesday he moved out. When she entered the house after work, she knew he was gone. The house was empty, a shell, and she felt loneliness envelop her as if the sun had disappeared from the universe. It had from hers.

The loneliness was short-lived. And she should have known. When Thane had said they'd get to know each other, he'd meant every word. Each evening, while Ronnie stayed at her house, Thane took her out. Night after night they saw Shreveport, every inch of it. They toured Fort Humbug, went to the symphony, went to the Barnwell Garden Center, ate catfish at the Cypress Inn and lobster at Don's. And every night Thane took her home early, kissing her passionately at her door and then saying good night, gathering up Ronnie and leaving her with mounting frustration. She knew she was on a collision course between her heart and her mind, the past and the future. She thought of two locomotives hurtling head-on down the same track, rushing toward each other. She felt as if her heart were in a race toward destruction.

She continued working on his patents, the carpenters continued working on his house, and he began manufacturing his game in the garage. The patents were feasible and Thane started to market the game while every night the tension boiled between them, threatening to explode. Standing in his arms when he kissed her was torment. She wanted more.

He hadn't said he loved her, but she had faced the fact that she loved him. Beyond her wildest dreams she loved him until it hurt so badly. She wanted to tell him, but she didn't know what he felt. The only certainty was, he would have to be the one to say good-bye. And she was sure he would someday. She couldn't shake the feeling of inadequacy. He was too much a man, too overwhelming and full of life to want a woman who was incomplete.

She saw that he could live in a predictable manner, or had she merely adjusted to his lifestyle? The only barrier left in her was that she might not be able to give him children, but how could she bring it up when he hadn't so much as mentioned love? He hadn't hinted at marriage. All he did was take her out, kiss her good night, and build a bomb of smoldering desire.

There wasn't an opportunity to bring up the subject of her health without sounding presumptuous, absurd. Mr. T. Prescott was as difficult to cope with as ever!

And she was determined to be in control of her emotions when she told him. She had to be strong enough to survive Thane's rejection with some kind of dignity. She could understand why he wouldn't want to marry her. At the moment he didn't seem inclined even to have an affair. She understood why he might reject her; she just couldn't cope with the knowledge.

Two weeks passed and her work began to show the strain. Her ability to concentrate was nil except on one subject. One blue-eyed subject.

At the office one morning in October she answered the phone to hear his deep voice.

"Working hard?"

"Trying."

"I'm trying too and finding it damned difficult. Laurel . . . Ronnie's in school."

Her breath went out in a long rush. "You changed your mind!"

"I decided to try, but so help me, if he comes home this afternoon in tears I can't send him back." She could hear the tenseness and the worry in his tone.

"I don't think he'll be in tears. He has too much of his father in him."

Silence. Then, "I'm so tough?"

"No, you're a cyclone, remember? You're a force all in and of yourself. You don't have to withstand other forces, you make your own."

"That's what you think. Do you know how much withstanding I've been doing these past few weeks?"

Pleasure filled her. "I have an idea how much."

"Want to come hold my hand at three o'clock?"

She smiled. He was so vulnerable where Ronnie was concerned. This tough, dynamic man had his weak spot and she didn't blame him. "If you need me."

"I need you far more than at three o'clock and I want far more than your hand," he answered in a husky drawl and her heart began pounding like wind-racked surf. "We know each other pretty well now."

The roaring in her ears drowned out everything except his voice, his deep, scratchy tone. "Your favorite color is blue," he went on, "you like fried chicken, hamburgers, chocolate sodas. You love to read, to garden, to ski. You live in a monastery like a nun."

"You can't call our good-byes nunlike."

"Almost. Well, I'll let you know what happens when my son comes home."

"Please do and don't worry. He's a chip off the old block." They hung up, but her small capacity for work had diminished to nothing. Ronnie's big blue eyes haunted her. She paced the floor, watched the clock, and worked herself into a dither before the phone finally rang late in the afternoon.

"Laurel?" Thane's deep voice conveyed his satisfaction and she let out her breath.

"How'd it go?"

"He's in the tree house now. He came in talking about the seashell collection the teacher had. He brought a shell home to show me and he'll take it back tomorrow. Ah, parenthood!"

She had an opening. Her hands knotted into fists. Tell him, she thought. Tell him now, quickly. Just say, "I can't be a parent. . . ."

"Thane, speaking of parenthood . . ."

But as if he hadn't heard, he went on blithely. "I'm demolished while he's happy as a lark. Honey, thanks."

The words were diamonds and gold. They were so precious to her that she forgot her confession. "You're welcome."

"He wanted a snack and then he sailed out to see Manuel and climb the tree. He's fine."

"I knew he would be. He's part you."

"The day started getting nice thirty minutes ago. I expect it to get a lot better in about four hours."

"Thane, there's something I have to tell you," she said breathlessly.

"Tell me tonight, hon."

She listened with relief and consternation as he continued, "Laurel, tomorrow I'm leaving to fly to Chicago to talk to the people at the Rayburn Toy Company. They're interested in Bzzip. I'll be back Wednesday."

"You think they'll manufacture the robot?"

"It sounds interesting. We'll see."

"Why don't you let Ronnie stay at our house while you're gone?"

"His grandmother, Pam's mother, is coming to stay with him. I want her to meet you."

She felt pleased and worried at the same time. The moment of truth was approaching and with it, probably rejection.

"In the meantime, we have tonight," he said.

"I'm happy about Ronnie. Thanks for calling to tell me."

"Sure. See you tonight." The phone clicked and she replaced it. Fear of the future definitely outweighed relief.

That night they went out, repeating the same frustrating pattern, and there wasn't any good opportunity to tell him. Thane kissed her good night and left town the next day. And a strange silence descended.

Like old sailors whose bones ache three days before rain, Laurel was developing her own signals of an approaching storm.

Thane hadn't said good-bye. He wasn't in town. He hadn't contacted her. As Wednesday came and went without a word from him, with every bone in her body she could feel something brewing in the wind.

On Friday afternoon she walked around the block and spent an hour with Ronnie and Mrs. Haskins, Thane's mother-in-law from Cleveland. She learned two things: one, that Thane was traveling and would be home soon; two, that each day he talked with Ronnie several times at great length. Dismayed that he hadn't called her once since he left, she went home in shock. She felt deserted. And realized he was an unpredictable as ever and it was still difficult for her to accept.

When the storm finally broke, it came with a very special warning. The following Tuesday morning, one week and a day since Thane had left Shreveport, she rose, gazed at her wardrobe, rummaged in the back of the closet, and pulled out a dress she hadn't worn for years. A bright red silk dress. Let her brothers faint when she reached the office. It gave her spirits a lift and with Thane gone, she needed one.

She bathed, washed her hair, started to knot it, and stopped. Carefully, she brushed it and let it fall free, hanging to her waist, the long black and silky strands swirling slightly when she walked.

At the office, only Marie had a definite reaction to Laurel's appearance. To Jordan and Lamont, she was their little sister whether her hair was up or down. After thanking Marie for her compliments, she went to her office and sat down to work.

She had the drawings and specifications spread before her for Mr. V. York's car vacuum, when she heard a strange clanking and whirring, and then Jordan yelling, "What the hell?"

Puzzled, she hurried out into the hall where she almost fell over Bzzip. The robot stopped, raised a hand, and held out a note.

"What is that?" Jordan asked, frowning. Lamont emerged from his office to look at the scene.

Her pulse developed a new beat, twice as fast as the old one. "It's Bzzip," she answered without thinking, taking the note and reading the scrawling handwriting: "I need your love. The clouds are beginning to gather. Take shelter—'Cyclone.' P.S. I'm in the front talking to Marie."

"Prescott, no doubt," Jordan said dryly and disappeared into his office.

Lamont walked around the robot. "That's dammed interesting. Is this one of his inventions?"

She forgot to answer. She reread, "The clouds are beginning to gather," and her heart told her, here comes a dilly of a storm! Joyously, she said, "Get out your umbrella, Lamont."

"My umbrella? There's not a cloud in the sky. What's the matter with you?"

"It's raining, Lamont. It's pouring in torrents." She picked up Bzzip and walked down the hall.

Thane was sitting with one hip on the corner of Marie's broad oak desk. He wore a charcoal suit which gave him such a debonair, handsome look that Laurel's heart constricted violently. His back was to her. One hand held the control box for Bzzip, the tanned fingers resting on his thigh. Below his mass of thick brown curls a narrow expanse of bronzed neck showed above his collar.

As if he felt her presence, he stood up and turned to her. She saw the impact of his blue eyes. They darkened to stormy depths as he slowly, thoroughly took in her clinging red dress, her long, flowing hair.

From behind, she heard Lamont say, "There's not a drop of rain! Is that thing yours, Prescott?" Lamont collided into her back, an action so uncharacteristic of him that she was dumb-founded. But only for one tiny second, and then she realized the cyclone was beginning to blow. Or the Pied Piper had started to whistle his magic tune. Either way, the result was bound to be devastation.

"I'm fine, Lamont," Thane answered, then blinked. A startled look crossed his face. And if she hadn't felt so confused, so stunned by his sudden appearance, she would have laughed. His answer to Lamont's question was as ridiculous as some of hers had been to his questions in the past.

"Gee whiz!" he breathed. "Holy white whiskers!"

As befuddled and bemused as he, she answered, "Gee whiz, yourself!"

"You let your hair down."

Lamont spoke in a louder than normal tone. "If you don't mind, I'll go out and take a look."

Vaguely, Laurel wondered what Lamont was talking about. She really didn't care.

"I want to look at some land," Thane said. "I made a nice deal with the Rayburn people to market Bzzip. I'll use the money to build a plant to manufacture my game. Can you come with me to look at a site?"

"Now?"

He nodded. She wondered if she could do anything except fling her arms around him. It was so good to see him. She had missed him badly. She didn't want to think about the time when she would tell him good-bye forever. She wouldn't think about it now. "Let me get my purse."

"You do that."

As she walked down the hall, out from under the spell of those bewitching blue eyes, her mind began to function again. Where had Lamont gone?

What did he want to look at? She began to get a shivery feeling. Cyclone, indeed!

She picked up her purse, looked at the papers spread on her desk, reached over and turned out the light, and left without looking back.

Thane took her arm and they stepped outside. Filling the lot was a strange-looking vehicle like a winged tricycle, made of aluminum tubing with wings of bright yellow sailcloth. Lamont leaned over it, looking at the controls.

"What on earth?" Laurel said.

"An ultralight," Thane answered. "It's the closest thing to wings, to being a bird. Come on. I'll show you."

She eyed the two small seats. "I can't ride in that thing. I'm in a dress."

"So Shreveport gets to see some pretty legs. Give the town a thrill."

He took her hand and they crossed the parking lot. Marie and Jordan followed them.

Lamont looked up. "How'd you get this here?"

"I can land or take off in fifty feet. I landed in the vacant lot behind this building and we'll take off the same way. There's enough clearance."

"Who built it?" A grudging respect was in Lamont's tone.

"This is my own design."

Laurel listened to the exchange in a daze. She was going to fly with Thane in a contraption of bits of wire and cloth. She glanced up at his mass of dark curls, his broad shoulders, his marvelous features, and worries about the machine vanished.

"What's it weigh?" Lamont stepped out of Laurel's way.

"Two hundred pounds. Costs me around five dollars an hour to fly."

"What fun, Laurel!" Marie exclaimed, her green eyes glittering with eagerness.

"You go in the back seat unless you want to fly this," Thane said.

"I can't ride in this dress."

"Sure you can." He held her hand while she sat down only inches above the paving. She buckled up. Pulling at her full red skirt, she tried to tug it down to cover her knees. Thane sat in front of her, scooting back between her knees. He picked up Bzzip and thrust him at Jordan.

"Jordan, buddy, would you keep an eye on my little friend for a while. I'll pick him up later."

A startled Jordan hugged Bzzip to his chest. "Why, certainly."

Laurel gave up trying to tuck her skirt under her. Of all days to decide to let her hair down and wear a flimsy skirt! She locked her arms around Thane's waist and pressed against his back. In a box behind her was a tiny engine, the blades beyond the engine. She said in his ear, "I'm not sure I want to do this."

"You will."

Confidence he did not lack. The motor started, the blades began to whir. This was going to carry her over Shreveport?

It did, in a magical ride that made her feel like a bird. At one high point, Thane cut the motor and they drifted, swooping, hearing sounds from below, while she clung to him and let her hair blow wildly behind her.

"It's wonderful!" she cried.

"I love you," he said, and then she really flew, her heart soaring for a moment while she let go of reality as easily as she had left the solid ground below. Later she could face the grim facts. Not now. He twisted slightly to wrap his arm around her and squeeze her. The wind buffeted her, as she gazed at him with longing.

"Of all places to tell me!"

His dimple appeared. "I'll tell you again." The ultralight dipped and he straightened to turn on the motor.

Dazzled, refusing to face anything unpleasant at the moment, she gloried in his declaration of love. She flew on wings of love with a strong wind carrying her through a cloudless sky.

As she looked down at the roofs below, the tall pines, she wondered where he planned to build. In the piney country, to the east, to the west? "Where'll you build?"

"In Denver," he called over his shoulder.

Ten

Shock burst her bubble of dreams. "Are we flying this contraption to Denver?"

He laughed. "No, there's our destination. My plane's there."

She looked below at the airport looming into sight. " '*My plane*'?" There were still some things she didn't know about the unpredictable Mr. T. Prescott! Her heart thumped and a tight knot formed. "Are you moving from Shreveport?"

"Yes."

Just like that. It was all taken out of her hands. He would move away. She didn't have to tell him no, explain why she couldn't be what he expected. He was ready to pack and go. Then why the hell did he tell her he loved her?

She glared at the mass of thick brown curls in front of her. "I can't go to Denver!"

"Why not?" he shouted.

Why not, indeed. Follow the Pied Piper . . . into the sea. Suddenly she let go of questions, of hesitation, of sorrow. Thane would disappear out of her life soon enough.

So he flew his own plane, a bright blue and white Beechcraft, to Denver and she went along, feeling dazed, listening to him talk about his plans for his own toy company.

They landed in Denver and while she gazed out tall glass windows at the mountains in the distance, Thane rented a jeep. She had stopped asking why he did anything. After they ate some fried chicken for lunch, he went to a department store.

When they stopped in front of a counter of sweaters, she asked, "Do I need jeans?"

The burning gaze that drifted over her red dress gave her her answer before he said, "No, your red dress is perfect." He purchased a thick, gray cardigan and handed it to her. "You'll want this, though."

When he climbed behind the wheel to drive toward the mountains, all she could think about was the fact that he planned to leave Shreveport soon—and he hadn't kissed her.

Together, the two caused a desperate longing to build up inside her, a yearning that threatened to engulf her.

After leaving Denver, they turned off the busy highway, taking a rough, winding road up a mountain. A few houses dotted the area, then the road became rougher and the houses disappeared. Beside the road there were only tall, straight aspen with their shimmering golden and rust-colored leaves, and pungent blue spruce. It was the middle of the afternoon, the warmest part of the day, and shafts of sunlight filtered to the ground wherever there was an opening between the trees. Curious about their destination, she glanced at Thane, noticing his firm jaw and determined look.

She was sitting next to the Pied Piper and he was whistling a magic tune. What was he up to? Wearing the gray sweater, she clutched the jeep as it bounced. The road was a mere path and they were up high where the air was rarified. As rarified as it always was in his presence. Was he building his plant on the mountaintop? It would be some drive to work for his employees!

"Don't you think this is a little inaccessible for a factory?" she shouted at him above the wind and the roar of the jeep.

He smiled. She clutched the seat to avoid being thrown out. The air was cold in the shade, warm in the sun. Remorse changed to anger and dismay. The man was crazy to build a factory up here.

Finally, he stopped. After he cut the motor the silence was intense, broken only by the sound of the wind sighing through the blue-green needles of the spruce trees, the faint, whispery rustle of shimmering aspen leaves as they clung their last days to white branches.

They were on top of the mountain. And she was on top of the world. She had to come down and the moment was approaching swiftly. She loved him, but he was as unpredictable as ever and this was still unsettling her. How unsettling? How important was she to him? What difference would her inadequacies make to him? She said a quick, silent prayer that she was strong enough to survive the descent from her mountaintop.

Through the trees she could see a breathtaking view of other mountains. Beside her was the most breathtaking sight—Thane. He lifted her out of the jeep and for the first time, she noticed a small trunk beneath an aspen. Black shiny metal with brass fittings, the trunk looked incongruous in the wild setting. And she noticed something else. Two tall pines had been cut down recently, leaving a small patch of sunny, cleared land.

Thane crossed to the trunk and knelt to open it, his dark slacks pulling tautly over his long legs. He shook out a green wool blanket and laid it on the ground, then produced a bottle of champagne and two glasses. Laurel blinked in amazement. A shaft of sunlight splashed over Thane's brown hair as he stood beside the tall pine trees and aspens and poured the champagne. A dreamlike quality enveloped her and she walked closer. The trunk was filled with an odd assortment—jeans, a sweat shirt, boots, a mysterious gray box. He shuffled through them, stirring them up, to pull out another blanket.

The blankets began to make her nervous. "What are you doing?" she asked, overcome with curiosity.

He straightened and turned around, his gaze locking with hers. An invisible wind roared in her ears. She read the answer in blue, his startling blue eyes.

He placed his hands on her shoulders, lifting the heavy hair away from her face, and his voice was a heart-stopping husky rasp. "I love you, Laurel."

Standing still, dressed in a red silk dress, facing Thane in his charcoal suit and dark tie, surrounded by a wilderness, her heart shattered into a thousand crystal fragments. A primitive longing tore through her, a timeless need. She realized he intended to take her here, to make her his. She knew without a word being spoken. And her heart responded, roared in her ears and went up in scarlet, dancing flames.

And then he surprised her.

He rubbed his thumb along her jaw and in his deep voice, asked, "Will you marry me?"

At the moment it was the last thing she expected him to say. Fighting pain, caught off guard, she answered honestly, "I don't know. . . ."

"Why not?"

His eyes were like shards of ice, cutting into her to lay her heart bare. Her breathing became difficult. She blinked rapidly, thrown off balance by his abrupt question. "You have a unique way of proposing! What happened to love and kisses?"

And the ice melted. A mocking, determined glint replaced it. "I intend to get to that."

She took a step backward. His voice was soft as he reached for her and pulled her into his arms. "You told me once that you couldn't take love lightly. That's good. Because I'm going to make you mine, Laurel. I won't let you say no. I want commitment from you. Absolute, total." His voice deepened to a hoarse, seductive whisper that flitted across her senses like fireflies dancing in a dark night. "I'm going to kiss you, to love you until you agree. I bought this land for our home."

Her eyes flew wide open. "Our home!"

"It'll give us a new start away from old memories. Together here, we can make our own. I bought this for you."

She was overcome. A sweeping, aching need for him engulfed her. It no longer mattered how unpredictable he was, how unconventional his lifestyle. There was only one stumbling block left.

"Thane, I can't . . ."

His head dipped, his mouth captured hers, and an incredible blaze burst between them. His demanding tongue thrust into her mouth relentlessly, clashing with hers, demanding her full response. How long she had waited! White heat raged through her loins as she pressed against his hard, marvelous body?

His arms crushed her; he tore his mouth away. "Why say you can't? What is it, Laurel?"

His blue eyes pinned her, as his big hand cupped

her head. She had to tell him, no matter how badly it hurt. Her voice was breathless. "I'm just not enough for you. . . ."

His strong baritone was filled with tenderness as he held her and kissed her cheeks. "Because you can't have children?" he said gently. "It doesn't matter."

Of all the shocks he had given her, this was the biggest. It was heart-stopping, monumental! Stunned, she pulled away to look up at him, whispering, "You know?"

He placed his big hands on both sides of her face as he looked into her eyes. "Honey, I saw you holding Ronnie that first night. I saw the tears on your cheeks. We were strangers, so you wouldn't cry like that over Ronnie. I finally guessed. And, Laurel, I want you."

She didn't dare hope. She felt as if her heart and lungs had ceased to function. A deep, urgent longing erupted within her. "You love children, toys, you're too full of life. I'm not enough for you—"

"Oh, Laurel! Without you I only half exist!" His voice was rough, throaty. "I've stayed away from Shreveport. When I was there, I saw you constantly. I know what I want."

"You've known all this time?" She was still reeling with shock. "Why did—"

"Why did I wait? You said we needed to get to know each other."

And the first sprout of hope blossomed. He had known all along, been patient enough to take her out constantly. . . . It was difficult to talk, but she said, "I lost a baby in a miscarriage when I was in my fifth month. It was after Wade's death. I was in bed through most of the pregnancy and according to the doctor in California, I may not be able to have children."

While she talked, his thumbs stroked her cheeks, brushing away the tears that spilled over. When she finished, she focused on his chin.

"Laurel." She raised her eyes to meet his. Blue, that gorgeous blue she had noticed the first moment they met, took command of her heart. He spoke quietly and with the firmness of steel. "Laurel. We have Ronnie. There are alternatives. It doesn't matter."

"Yes, it does," she cried.

He shook his head. "No. Not as much as my need for you. I'm not complete without you. I've been so lonely. I need you for Ronnie too." He leaned down to kiss her. His arms tightened and his mouth conveyed his determination, his love.

"C'mon, babe, let go of the last little bit of fear. Take a chance on life, on me," he said.

So she did. She wound her arms around his neck, heedless of her salty tears mingling with his kisses as she laughed and cried and kissed him. "I love you, Thane!"

"It's damn well high time! Will you marry me?"

"Oh, yes!" A fabulous cyclone carried her away from all her caution. She pulled his head down and met his mouth in a duel that made fires dance in the whirlwind.

He molded her to his long, hard body. He slipped the sweater off her shoulders and flung it away, his lips leaving hers long enough for him to whisper, "Tell me if you get cold."

"I don't think I'll ever be cold again."

His arms tightened and his tongue thrust into her warm mouth. Winding her fingers in his soft curls, she relished their sensual tickle, then slipped her hands lower to push the elegant coat off his shoulders. It dropped on pine needles in a heap, unnoticed. He trailed kisses along her throat. "Do you know what those damned pure good night kisses cost me?"

She stood on tiptoe to kiss his ear, his warm throat, feeling the tiny bristles of his beard. "I know exactly. What do you think they did to me? And I really wouldn't describe them as 'pure.' "

He looked down at her and his eyes burned with blue heat. Carefully, he parted her hair, lifting it over her shoulders so he could reach the zipper at her neck. While his eyes held her, causing a shower of golden sparks, his fingers tugged down her zipper and cool air rushed over her bare skin.

She reached up to unfasten his tie, moving her fingers lovingly against his throat, trembling in urgency as she undressed him.

His hands pushed the red silk over her shoulders, a scarlet flame undulating, drifting down over pale curves of shoulder and hip and calf to her ankles. At a more languorous pace, his gaze followed, lowering to make her flesh spring into tantalizing awareness, to stretch her nerves raw.

Her heart pounded until she felt it would burst with anticipation, with love, with joy. She pushed away his shirt, nesting her hand on his broad chest that she had ached to touch for oh, so many nights now!

He held her away from him and she saw hunger, and happiness in his eyes, his silent, sure message of love. She felt as if she were on the brink of a profound discovery, as if all of life were beckoning with a promise of newness, of completion. His broad, muscular shoulders made her ache, an exquisite agony that swept through her like a tidal wave, building, looming larger as it gained a surging power.

A violent trembling seized her. She wanted him so desperately. She longed to love him with abandon. She undressed him with fingers as shaky as his. Until she peeled away his charcoal slacks.

"Oh, my heavens!"

"I wore them just for you."

The damned tiger-striped underwear! And they looked just as sexy as she thought they would. "Now I know why I burned the eggs!"

They both laughed, then looked deeply into each other's eyes and amusement vanished, along with the underwear and her filmy lace underthings. All were strewn aside over pine needles and rocks. She wanted to love every inch of his hard virile body, yet his hands, his mouth on hers, made her close her eyes, gasp with pleasure as she yielded to him.

He pulled her down on the blanket. She felt the thick wool scratch her shoulder blades, calves, and buttocks, then she felt only the erotic roughness of his solid thighs. Thane captured her attention fully, kneeling beside her as he drank in her beauty, studying her long pale legs, her raven hair fanned out behind her head. She trailed her fingertips up his thigh over short, crisp hairs, the faint lines of scars, to his flat stomach. He was a dream breathed into life, into a hard, powerful reality. He gasped and leaned down to cup a full breast in his big palm, his rough fingers rubbing across the eager, rosy peak. She melted into a molten, feminine response to his male claim.

Then he stretched out beside her, pulling her against his length, his tumescent male arousal pressing her warm thigh as he kissed her hotly.

She felt his restraint, the leashed power of his desire.

"Laurel, now I can love you like I've wanted to for so long." He bent over and kissed each taut, quivering nipple, brushing and teasing while her hands lavished caresses on his broad powerful back, exulting in his smooth flesh, the narrow tapering at his waist, his hipbones.

His rough fingers trailed boldly up the inside of her silken thighs, compounding her need, tarrying to explore. His big hands searched, discovered her body, her honeyed warmth, the ways to excite her, to drive her beyond thought until she gasped and clung to him. And while his fingers practiced their own magic persuasion, her heart sang with love.

"Thane . . . Thane," she whispered, glorying in the wonder of his love. The soft whimpers in her throat were lost on the wind as she feasted her gaze on his magnificent body. The moment became a celebration to her, a promise of fulfillment, recompense for a lost, lonely life.

His dark head moved lower, the mass of curls tickling her flesh as his tongue sent fiery trails across her belly. She quivered with longing as steamy tension coiled, tightening inside her.

She moved indolently, her limbs heavy, her breath fluttering. "Thane, I've waited . . ."

She knelt beside him while he sat and faced her. She cupped his face in her hands and leaned forward slowly to kiss him, to convey the unfathomable stormy desire she felt, the boundless joy.

His hands sought and found her full breasts, kneading gently, pressing them to him. His strong arms enfolded her, but she slipped free, her kisses trailing over his coppery skin. Her dark hair cascaded across his bronze shoulders, on her pale flesh, the long strands slipping away as her head lowered. She kissed the flat male nipples and heard his forceful intake of breath. Her lips sought his hard stomach, grazing taut muscles, sharp hipbones.

A shudder racked him as his fingertips dallied over her nape, her back. His deep, hoarse voice groaned her name again and again as if the cry came from his soul.

She answered with her hands, her lips, her heart. She stroked his maleness, kissed him, and knew his control had burned away.

Gathering her in his arms, he returned her passionate kisses, then moved her beneath him, shifting her legs apart. She felt incredibly starved, wracked with desire, so radiantly alive.

He paused over her, his blue eyes devouring her with a primordial hunger.

"Laurel, how I've needed you. . . . I'll make you mine forever, as long as we both shall live. . . ."

Her heart threatened to burst with love. Wildfire licked her limbs as her hips lifted toward him, seeking his maleness, seeking completion.

He lowered his body between her legs, thrust inside her, and she arched in response.

In a swift flash of insight, she knew this was what she had wanted since that moment he had turned to face her, the first night when she had unzipped the silly gorilla suit and found the man beneath. In that moment, a magic attraction had sparked to life between them. And later, in the kitchen when he had kissed her, he had taken her heart. She wanted him, loved him, and now he loved her in return.

They lay beneath the dark pines, their soft moans of love tangling with the windsong of fluttering leaves and green needles, low sounds drifting over the mountaintop into the air, while the song that lasted was silent, heart-to-heart, from each to the other. Her arms circled his body, a slender lock that held him to her heart while she moved with him, as sensation after sensation pounded her senses, drummed through her system to drive her beyond thought into a world of feeling, of flaming desire.

A high cry of delight was flung on the wind, followed by another as their movements became frenzied and he drove her to another peak, to completion, to paradise.

Her body tightened, her knees pressing his hips as she shook violently, surging to a climax that brought ecstasy. She gave herself to him, heart, body, mind, and soul. He took her gift and gave his own—completion. A union that forged a link forever between them, stronger than steel, eternal.

Thane shuddered in release, his big body pulsating with satisfaction, giving her rapture.

Oblivion followed sensation. She held him close, relishing his weight pressing her to the hard ground, the solid feel of his marvelous body. She gasped for breath, feeling dewey, bewitched, estactic. His own breath was against her warm throat. She felt his arm move slightly as he reached across her. And then she heard bells.

Her eyes flew open. Bells tinkled in the fresh mountain air, melodic bells playing a tune she had heard one other time. She shifted slightly to find amused, adoring blue eyes watching her.

"What on earth? Where are those bells?"

He raised slightly, leaving her warmth, rolling away to stretch beside her as he held up a small dancing bear. Bells tinkled as it turned.

"Ronnie's toy?"

" 'The damned bells,' is what you said that first day. And when you did, I knew you felt the same attraction I did." His eyes worshiped her, lingering over her features as if he were memorizing her. "I think I fell in love when these bells played that September afternoon in my yard. I couldn't resist bringing them up here."

How could such a wonderful man love her? Her throat felt tight and her eyes burned.

"Hey! No tears today. I won't allow it."

"I love you," she whispered and his blue eyes darkened. "You planned this for me. You bought this lot and came up here ahead of time. . . ." He leaned down to kiss her and reaffirm what they saw in each other's eyes.

He raised and stretched one bare arm across her, rubbing her pink nipples, bringing them to a taut awareness instantly. He placed a small box on her breast.

"I brought this too."

She looked down at the blue box, rising and falling as she breathed. Her curiosity was offset by the coppery arm and hand on her stomach. She picked up his hand and kissed his palm.

"Thank you. This is the best gift of all."

She heard his quick drawing of breath. He sat up and the sunlight splashed over his bronze shoulders, catching the auburn glints in his tight curls. He pulled her up to kiss her hotly, passion flaring between them as her breasts thrust against his broad, furred chest.

After a moment he raised his head, retrieved the box and opened it. He withdrew a huge, sparkling diamond and slid it on her finger.

Accompanied by the fresh scent of pine and the light touch of a breeze across the mountain, his husky voice strummed over her nerves, starting a new chorus of need as he said, "With this ring, I thee love forever, beyond world and time. . . ."

And blue eyes, blue wizardry enchanted her, holding her spellbound as his strong brown arms pulled her to his big, thudding heart.

Laurel stood in Thane's arms by the kitchen

window while he kissed her throat. She held him, never tiring of the feeling of his big, broad shoulders under her hands. "Mmmm," she murmured, ". . . and where is Ronnie?"

"Out chasing rabbits. I saw him start down the mountain," Thane murmured as his lips moved closer to hers. She looked up at him, brushing his curls away from his forehead.

"And Trish?"

"She's in the backyard."

Laurel sighed. "Thane, I wish we could have had one more."

"Shh. We have a wonderful family. If we had a choice, we couldn't go through that again. I couldn't."

"It was worth all the trouble." She thought about the long months of lying in bed, staying off her feet until the caesarean delivery.

"We have our son and our daughter. She's perfect, a copy of her mother," he said as he ran his hand down Laurel's spine, sending a shower of sparks flying after his touch. His big hands rested on her hips, pulling her jeaned thighs against his.

"Oh, I don't know about that."

"She has beautiful gray eyes and black hair. . . ."

"Very curly black hair." She touched his bristly chin, thinking how good the years had been to her. Thane's toys were successful. He had a large toy company. They had their house, a rustic home high on the mountain. She had followed her Pied Piper into paradise. She glanced out the window at their backyard, the spruce and aspen on the mountain around them. Her eyes narrowed as she saw a curly black head move into sight. "She has a little of her daddy in her too."

"You think so?" He nuzzled her throat, bending

down to reach lower as tingles radiated from his kisses.

"Take a look."

Thane straightened and glanced out the window. "Oh, my God!" Boots clattering, he dashed for the door.

Laurel laughed, humming a tune as she watched with amusement. A small girl dressed in Ronnie's old red cape and blue Superman outfit slowly climbed a ladder toward the garage roof. Tucked beneath her arm was a folded yellow umbrella. Laurel smiled, knowing Thane would get there in time to catch Trish. Then suddenly she paused and looked again. Drawing a quick breath, she ran for the door. Since when could she predict how a cyclone would act?

She'd better get out there—just in case he intended to show his daughter the proper way to parachute off the garage!

THE EDITOR'S CORNER

Imagine the dark night sky on the Fourth of July with myriad fireworks going off—exciting skyrockets buzzing through the air, and wheels of dazzling colors exploding in the dark heavens. We've tried to give you a LOVESWEPT celebration for Independence Day that matches those fireworks in exciting and beautiful reading entertainment.

To start our July "display" we have another real dazzler from Sandra Brown in LOVESWEPT #51, **SEND NO FLOWERS.** As always, Sandra gives us a wonderfully satisfying love story. Do you remember the dear, clinging Alicia from **BREAKFAST IN BED,** LOVESWEPT #22? She was the lady who inadvertently caused the torment that kept Sloan and Carter apart. Well, now Sandra has had Alicia grow up and become an independent woman and an excellent mother for her two boys. Still, though, love has eluded Alicia. But, in **SEND NO FLOWERS,** Alicia meets the man she's never even dared to dream of finding. Alicia has taken her sons on a camping trip when a violent thunderstorm blows up. Just what a mother alone needs, right? Then the devastatingly attractive and gently caring Pierce Reynolds charges to the rescue. Just what a mother alone needs, for sure! Pierce not only saves the family's camping trip, but brings a completeness to Alicia's life that she has never known before. Pierce has a terrible secret, though, and it threatens his and Alicia's new found love. The conclusion of this shimmeringly sensual love story is so highly dramatic and emotionally touching that I suspect you w remember **SEND NO FLOWERS.**

(continued)

(#53)

Isn't it interesting to read a love story that's the product of a collaboration between a happily married husband and wife? Think back to **LIGHTNING THAT LINGERS** by Sharon and Tom Curtis, for example. I trust you'll find a special quality of romance in Liv and Ken Harper's first romance for us, **CASEY'S CAVALIER**, LOVESWEPT #52. In this charming book, heroine Casey O'Neil pulls every trick in the book to evade process server Michael Cooper . . . even to faking a heart attack and donning clever disguises. She'll stop at nothing to keep from appearing in court. But nowhere has there ever been a more determined (or heroic!) pursuer than Michael. (He's quite a determined wooer, too!) Casey's and Michael's zany pursuit toward love is like a string of firecrackers going off in this fast-paced love story. You've read the romances by Liv and Ken under the pseudonyms of Jolene Adams (SECOND CHANCE AT LOVE) and JoAnna Brandon (ECSTASY) and now you can enjoy **CASEY'S CAVALIER** published at last under their real names.

You've heard me say it before, but it bears repeating: it's an enormous pleasure for editors to find a brand-new writing talent and publish an author for the very first time. Making her debut as a published author next month is Barbara Boswell with LOVESWEPT #53, **LITTLE CONSEQUENCES**. In this delectable romance Shay Flynn knows that blueblood lawyer Adam Wickwire would make a perfect father for the baby she longs to have . . . but marriage is out of the question—for poignant reasons. So, she makes up her mind to seduce Adam, then vanish forever from his life. When the weekend they spend together leaves her breathless—and more than a little in love—Shay discovers that her perfect plan has resulted in some very, very interesting **LITTLE CONSEQUENCES!**

A month with a romance by Joan Domning is a month with an extra ray of sunshine! In LOVESWEPT #54, **THE GYPSY AND THE YACHTSMAN,** Joan has outdone herself once more. When heroine Tanya Stanchek's horoscope predicts that "romance will crash into you," she hasn't a clue it's going to happen . . . literally! Then a speeding car smacks into hers and tosses the ruggedly handsome Gene Crandall into her path. But a charmingly offbeat fortuneteller, Madame Delores, a mysterious yachtsman whom Tanya has only glimpsed from afar, Gene's biases, and her own anxieties jeopardize the "destined" romance of these two wonderful people. Joan has brewed a delicious stew, seasoned with just the right spices and lots of touching emotion, and I'll bet you agree with me that this is one of her most creative "recipes" for love!

Have a wonderful month of lazy, happy July days brightened up even more by our LOVESWEPT "fireworks."

Warm regards,

Carolyn Nichols

Carolyn Nichols
  Editor
LOVESWEPT
Bantam Books, Inc.
666 Fifth Avenue
New York, NY 10103

LOVESWEPT

Love Stories you'll never forget by authors you'll always remember